SUDDENLY, A THREATENING SOUND SHATTERED THE QUIET . . .

Just past sunup, Slocum saw a broken sign pointing the way to the Spit Bucket Mine. He shook his head, wondering where the miners got their names. This claim hardly sounded worth the effort, yet he knew Hearst was willing to pay an incredible sum for both mines. From his brief check of the Silver Canary, it was valuable, but nowhere near worth three-hundred-fifty-thousand dollars. That meant the Spit Bucket had high-grade ore buried under its dilapidated sign.

Swinging out of the saddle, Slocum walked to the mouth of the mine. He froze when the ominous sound of a gun cocking echoed from the shaft.

"You take another step and I'll blow your damned head off your shoulders . . ."

JAKE LOGAN

VIRGINIA CITY SHOWDOWN

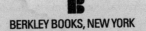

BERKLEY BOOKS, NEW YORK

VIRGINIA CITY SHOWDOWN

A Berkley Book / published by arrangement with
the author

PRINTING HISTORY
Berkley edition / March 1993

ISBN: 0-425-13761-9

A BERKLEY BOOK ® TM 757,375
Berkley Books are published by The Berkley Publishing Group,
200 Madison Avenue, New York, New York 10016.
The name "BERKLEY" and the "B" logo
are trademarks belonging to Berkley Publishing Corporation.

PRINTED IN THE UNITED STATES OF AMERICA

10   9   8   7   6   5   4   2   3   2   1

1

John Slocum looked up at the sheer red granite walls on either side of the trail from Silver City. The road had narrowed to a path and then even that pathetic rocky track had vanished. He knew he was still heading toward Virginia City from the evidence around him. Here and there he saw evidence of recent human passage. A piece of cloth, a spent brass cartridge shining in the hot summer sunlight, silvered nicks of shod horses' hooves against stone—it was all here.

The walls narrowed more as he made a turn in the canyon. He reined back and looked at the railroad trestle spanning the canyon three hundred feet above his head. He saw the smoke billowing from the locomotive's boilers before he heard the deep rumble as the long train crossed the bridge.

"Gold," he muttered to himself. "Bet that train's so loaded with gold the trestle's going to give way one day."

He had been down on his luck for longer than he cared to remember. Gambling hadn't gone well over in Reno. A try at silver mining had given him a sore back and nothing else to show for the long weeks spent in the horrendously

1

hot mine filled with water boiling up around his ankles. And this was the third horse he'd ridden in as many months. One had just upped and died, no reason that Slocum could see, and another had been stolen right out from under his nose.

"Grain, old boy," he said, patting the gelding on its neck. "That's what you're going to get when we hit it big in Virginia City. The Comstock Lode might not be as much as it was ten years back, but there'll be plenty for us. Gold, silver, it'll all be there."

The horse turned its head and looked at him with a big brown eye before snorting in disgust, as if saying Slocum was just blowing smoke.

"Let's go," Slocum said, urging the horse through the ravine. "We've a ways to go before Virginia City." He rode another ten minutes before he saw the barbed-wire fence running across the canyon. The only break in the fence was guarded by three men with shotguns. Slocum looked around, wondering if there was an easier way of getting through. Unless he sprouted wings and flew, he didn't see it. Going back to Silver City would mean another day's ride.

He approached the watchful men, moving so that his right hand rested near the ebony butt of his Colt Navy riding easy in its cross-draw holster. Slocum had no call getting involved in someone else's dispute, and that's what this looked to be.

"Afternoon, gents," he greeted. He touched the brim of his hat, pulling it down just enough to keep the light out of his eyes. If he had to shoot, he didn't want the bright Nevada sun blinding him.

"Welcome to Devil's Gate," the tallest of the three said. "This here's a toll gate."

"You mean I have to pay to ride along?" Slocum frowned. Fencing off range land was one thing, charging to cross it was another. He didn't much like this.

"Five dollars and you'll be in Virginia City by sundown." The tall man wiped at the sweat on his bald head before replacing his hat. "Don't pay and you got one, maybe two days hard riding ahead of you."

"Five dollars is about all I've got," Slocum lied. He had twice that, but he didn't like this kind of highway robbery. Putting on a bandanna and sticking up a stagecoach was at least honest thievery.

"So?" broke in another. "This is the land where everybody gets rich. Just ride on into the Comstock and poke your finger in the ground. Blue dirt, damnedest, richest claims you'll find on the face of the earth."

"If it's so generous, why aren't you out getting rich?" Slocum asked.

All three laughed and the tall man answered, "We got our own gold mine, and you're looking at it. Pay up or ride off. We don't much care what you do."

Slocum saw there wasn't any point in arguing. Shooting it out with the three would be foolish. The soft mounds of dirt in the otherwise hard ground a few yards off showed where they had planted others with a mind to fight over their toll. Slocum reached into his shirt pocket and found a slim wad of greenbacks. He peeled off five and stared at the two remaining. He had less money than he'd thought.

"Much obliged," the third man said, taking the money from Slocum. "Ride on through." The others pulled back their gate and allowed Slocum to ride on to what they'd made out to be the richest city on the face of the planet.

As Slocum approached Virginia City, he wasn't so sure. The whole damned town had burned down recently, maybe within the last six months. The acrid odor of charred timber made his nose twitch. The buildings, however, seemed in good condition, having been rebuilt quickly. A building high on the slope across the ravine from Virginia City—St. Mary's on the Mountain, Slocum read on a sign pointing toward the spired church—dominated the valley.

He urged his horse forward, noticing the crushed gravel on the road. A slow smile crossed his lips. He knew low-grade quartz ore when he saw it. They had paved the streets of Virginia City with gold!

If the town itself had been reduced by fire recently, the houses up on Gold Hill hadn't. He saw mansions that would have done any antebellum South plantation owner proud. White pillars and broad porches and huge glass windows stretched everywhere, the evidence of the real wealth in the steep-walled gorge that protected Virginia City. He put his heels to his gelding's flanks. The scent of riches replaced that of burned wood in his nostrils.

Slocum came to a fork in the road. One street angling off to the west had been used less than the one covered with the crushed quartz. On impulse, Slocum turned down the lesser path and came out on B Street. Evidence of the fire was more apparent here. Saloons had been partially burned and never reopened. Stores struggled to hold up weakened walls with rough-hewn timbers, and no structure had escaped unscathed.

He turned down a side street, heading a little downhill until he came to C Street. Slocum thought he had died and gone to heaven. Dozens of boisterous bawdy houses were running full, and it was hardly late afternoon. Saloons blared with loud music and the dull roar of men enjoying themselves came to him from all directions. Riding down the middle of the street, he studied both sides.

A large brick structure, Piper's Opera House at the corner of Union, advertised Lotta Crabtree's imminent arrival to sing for all and sundry. A block farther east stood another impressive brick building. The Melodian boasted a troupe of Red Stocking Blondes and the chance for some lucky patron to win a free silver brick during every intermission. For all the promise this entertainment held for Slocum, he turned to the saloons lining the street.

He'd always heard there was a whiskey mill every fifteen steps in Virginia City, and now he believed it. There were more than he could choose from. The Sawdust Corner looked promising, but the crowd inside was gathered around a pit where two dogs fought. Slocum looked for other diversion. He kept riding, eyeing the Sazarac and the Crystal Bar and finally decided the Howling Wilderness was his kind of place.

Inside the saloon, he stopped to let his eyes adjust to the dimness. Lamps burned at the corners of the room, filling it with cloying smoke that obscured the huge painting of a reclining nude woman behind the bar. Slocum didn't know much about art but decided he wouldn't mind meeting the woman who had posed for the picture.

"Something to wet your whistle, mister?" asked the barkeep, already reaching under the bar.

"How much for a bottle?" Slocum asked. He had been on the trail a long time but was all too aware of the few greenbacks rubbing together in his shirt pocket. The men at Devil's Gate had taken too much from him, but the notion of riding another two days didn't appeal to him.

"Twenty," the bartender said with hesitation, as if this new robbery was the way he usually did business. And it might have been. Slocum saw huge piles of bills stacked on the green-felt-covered gaming tables. And the mounds of gold dust told him no matter how much a man might have, there was always just a bit more to be had.

"Beer," he said, pushing across one of his worn, folded greenbacks. The barkeep snorted and took it, not offering any change with the mug of weak local brew. Slocum had two dollars and a few coins to his name. That wasn't much—not nearly enough for a good game.

Slocum nursed the beer for almost fifteen minutes as he watched the card games around the saloon. The Howling Wilderness was mild compared to others, and that suited him just fine. This seemed a saloon where the miners came to quietly get drunk. Now and then the bouncer would make a pass through the huge room and grab the collar of anyone who'd passed out. Slocum wondered how much the bouncer made by robbing the drunk patrons after he threw them into the alley running out back of the bar.

He bided his time, even considering getting another beer when he saw his chance. A chair opened at a poker game, and he quickly sat down.

"Howdy, gents," he said, looking at the other five at the table. Two were drunk, one had to be propped up, another had a wild look to him, and the fifth sat stolidly, hardly looking up from the cards he clutched like a lifeline.

The one sober man to his immediate left put down his cards, pressing them down hard into the table as if someone might snatch them away. Cold eyes like frozen mud fixed on Slocum. It was obvious he didn't like what he saw. From the pile of greenbacks in front of him, Slocum knew why. He was busy fleecing the drunks and didn't want competition.

"Always room for one more," the man said insincerely.

"Good," Slocum said, getting his money out. The man to his left pulled his money back a little, as if Slocum were going to reach out and take some of it.

In spite of his small stake, Slocum didn't need to steal from the man. The drunks were more than happy to bet insanely, drawing to inside straights, being unsure if three of a kind beat a flush. What astounded Slocum most, was that the drunks didn't much care if they won or lost. He caught the almost-frantic need to boast of their riches.

Along with it, he got the feeling no one in the Howling Wilderness believed their good fortune would last much longer. After burning, Virginia City had been returned to its former glory, but Slocum guessed it might be for the last time. The vitality of the Comstock Lode was petering out. Another fire and the town might not get rebuilt.

Slocum played conservatively at first, then began to bet more aggressively as his stake grew. By now the sun had dipped behind Mount Davidson and the miners were pouring into town from their claims. The oil lamps were turned up and the smoke became so dense Slocum found himself choking and sweat running down his face.

The man to his left jerked his cards close to his chest, as if Slocum had tried to get a peek at his hand.

Between him and the man, they had cleaned out the drunk miners. Slocum looked him over and asked, "You want to do this right?"

"What do you mean?" Brown eyes fixed on Slocum, greed flaring.

"We each draw a card. High card wins everything."

Slocum saw the man going over odds in his head, and he saw the same desperation blaze in the man's face that had possessed the others. Live fast. Go for broke. Bet it all on a single draw of the cards.

"Think of the bragging rights you'll get with it, if you win," Slocum said, goading the man. He didn't say anything about how the man would feel if he lost.

"Suits don't mean squat," the man said loudly. "High card wins. If we tie, we draw again."

"Fair enough," Slocum said. He watched the man shuffle the deck of greasy cards, cut them, and shuffle some more. Shoving them over to Slocum, he gestured impatiently for action.

"Barkeep, a fresh deck," Slocum called loudly, drawing attention. "We got the biggest bet in town riding on this." Slocum kept from laughing when he saw the panic flare on the man's face. Neither of them had been cheating when they'd played with the drunk miners; there hadn't been any need. But Slocum had seen how the deck had been marked. Tiny nicks and cuts along the edge, put there by the man's ragged fingernails, clearly revealed every face card and all the aces.

"Wait, no," the man started. He swallowed hard when he saw they were the center of attention. Miners crowded close, making side bets on who'd win. Slocum took the fresh deck and fanned them out, riffled through them to be sure they weren't marked also, then shuffled quickly.

"You want to cut?" Slocum asked.

The man licked dried lips and grabbed. He showed a queen. A slow smile spread over his face.

Slocum betrayed no emotion as he reached out. He had come into the Howling Wilderness with damned little. He might leave with nothing more than the weak beer in his belly, but he felt Lady Luck standing at his shoulder.

The king of spades came out of the deck and covered the queen.

A cheer went through the saloon. Slocum was, for a moment, a celebrity. He called out, "Buy my friend a bottle of your best whiskey! He's one hell of a good gambler." This took the sting out of the man losing his poke. If anything, Slocum's words reflected some glory on him. He left the table to accept his reward for losing, and Slocum quickly left the saloon after paying the barkeep.

His belly grumbled from lack of food. He had been living on nothing more than beans and biscuits made from wormy flour for the past week. It was high time he spent some of his newfound money on some decent victuals.

He looked up and down C Street at the two- and three-story brick buildings. At the far end of the street rose a whitewashed church and next to it sat a small café. Slocum headed for it, his belly grumbling the closer he got to his goal.

The dimly lit interior was crammed with tables decked out with linen cloths, spotless silverware, and the most wondrous smells he could remember sniffing. Slocum swallowed hard when he looked at the prices on the snow-white sheet of paper passing as a menu. He had to tell himself he wasn't likely to find cheaper prices anywhere in Virginia City. This was still a boom town—or fancied itself as such. Wealth flowed smooth and clear like water over a river rock.

Diving into the sizzling steak he had ordered, Slocum finished half of it before turning his attention to the fried potatoes. He paused to gulp down coffee so hot it burned his tongue. But he didn't care. This was the best meal he'd eaten in more than a month, and he wanted it inside him as quick as possible.

Only when he'd finished the steak and had worked through most of a fresh peach cobbler did he look around him. A few of the patrons cast furtive glances in his direction, wondering what a man like him was doing in such a fine café. He was sorely in need of a bath and shave and probably smelled worse than his horse. Slocum ignored them. He had the money to pay for his meal, and his greenbacks were as good as anyone else's.

Two women caught his attention, though, and held it firmly. He thought they might be sisters, the blonde a year or two older than the auburn-haired woman. Neither was more than thirty and from their cultured good looks might even be in their early twenties. Dressed up in their fancy rigging, he wondered if they were on their way to some special occasion or if they always got decked out like this.

They chatted quietly, heads close together, though now and then the blonde cast him a sidelong look. Slocum sipped his coffee, letting the hot liquid slide down his gullet and puddle warmly in his belly. He was about as content as a cat with a saucer of cream, and his mind began dancing around what it would be like having one of those elegant ladies on his arm.

Slocum blinked twice when he realized it wasn't any daydream. The lovely blonde had risen and came over, her long skirts swishing softly as she moved. She looked down at him, her cornflower-blue eyes bright.

"Ma'am?" Slocum wasn't sure what to say, caught so unexpectedly between dream and reality.

"I need you," was all she said, but it was enough to turn Slocum speechless.

2

"I beg your pardon?" Slocum tried to cover his confusion. He had been thinking of the woman in very unmannerly terms. She was gorgeous and he'd been on the trail a long time. Her blunt statement had caught him completely unawares.

"You have the look of a man who lives by his . . . wits," she finished lamely. Her bright blue eyes fixed on the Colt Navy stuck in the cross-draw holster. The worn ebony butt told of long, hard, and successful use.

"I'm not a hired gun," Slocum said, regaining his wits. "If I may be of some service to you, I'll be happy to do what I can. But I don't kill for money."

It was the blonde's turn to be flustered. She blushed and hid her mouth with her delicate hand. She looked down to the floor and started to turn away. Her sister put a hand on her shoulder, keeping her from fleeing in her embarrassment.

"Please forgive her, sir," the auburn-haired woman said in a no-nonsense tone. "Poor Coreopsis lets her emotions run away with her at times, and she says unfortunate things. Accept our apologies."

"No offense taken, ma'am," Slocum said. He frowned a little and had to ask, "Coreopsis?"

"Our manners are being eroded by this awful frontier living, I fear," the darker-haired woman said. "I am Belle Flowers, and this is my sister Coreopsis Flowers."

"People call me Corey," she said almost shyly. She batted her long eyelashes at him, and Slocum wondered who he'd have to kill. He quickly introduced himself.

"We do need assistance," Belle went on, ignoring her sister. "And we are willing to pay handsomely for the aid." She came on as a brisk all-business woman, but Slocum saw strong emotions lurking just underneath the facade.

"Please, will you join me?" Slocum stood and held out the chair for first Corey and then Belle. The sisters sat quickly. Slocum saw the ripple of conversation pass through the café as people wondered what these refined ladies were doing with such an obvious ruffian.

Corey kept her eyes down to her lap where her fingers played with a delicate lace handkerchief. Belle did the talking and was obviously the one in command.

"We are quite wealthy, Mr. Slocum," she began. "Our father—" She paused for a moment, looking to her sister. The blonde began to sniff and dab at her eyes with her handkerchief.

"Is something wrong?" Slocum asked, puzzled.

"He passed away recently and left us several silver mines," Corey said, looking at him. She had dabbed away all her tears. "We miss him so terribly."

"You might have heard of him. Dalton Flowers?" asked Belle. She went on before Slocum had to admit he'd never heard of the man. "We are not in his league when it comes to negotiating with . . . with such evil men."

"Who might these 'evil men' be?" Slocum's green eyes flashed form one sister to the other and back. Something bothered him about their story, and he couldn't figure out what it was.

"Claim jumpers, Mr. Slocum, claim jumpers!" Belle spoke so loudly others in the café turned and stared. "They want to steal it all. We need someone who knows mines to help us."

"I'm no miner." He smiled ruefully, remembering his hours of backbreaking work for so little return.

"We need someone to protect our rights. Those bullies would take one look at you and turn tail and run like the craven swine they are!" Belle said hotly. "You probably wouldn't have to even draw your pistol."

"No, you wouldn't," Corey rushed on. "We're selling the mines. We just need protection until we have disposed of them and can be on our way to somewhere more civilized."

"We intend to go to San Francisco," Belle said, glaring at her sister as if this were a state secret and not to be shared. "It shouldn't take more than a few days, a week at the most, to sell the mines. They are quite rich, and we have many offers for them already."

"Can't say I ever thought of myself as a wet nurse for a silver mine," Slocum said, watching the women's reaction. Whatever he expected from this seeming reluctance on his part, he didn't get it. Belle and Corey worked together like a team of snake-oil salesmen, one picking up with a new argument when the other flagged.

"A foreman. You'd be our foreman!" Corey declared. A curl of blond hair dipped down across her forehead. She casually tossed her head back like a frisky filly to get it out of her eyes. The smile she gave him was enough to melt a glacier.

"And we would never consider asking you simply to do us a favor. We can pay well," Belle went on. "How does one hundred dollars sound?"

"A month?" Slocum said, surprised.

"Oh, no, for a week. Certainly we won't require your services longer than that. And if we do, well—" Belle chewed at her lower lip as if wrestling with a weighty problem.

"Go on, Belle. You're such a tightwad." Corey turned to Slocum and said, "We shall pay one hundred dollars in gold a week for as long as it takes to sell the mines. If it takes a month, so be it!"

"That's a mighty generous offer," Slocum said, "but I can't say I know anything about running a mine."

"We are not currently mining," Belle said. "Protect our claims—and us—and I'm sure there can be a bonus in it for you."

She stared boldly at him, and Slocum had no doubts what Belle Flowers meant. He wondered if it would live up to his daydreams. Glancing from Belle to Corey and back, he decided it probably would.

"You've got yourself a foreman," he said. The waiter came over with the bill. Slocum started to say something about robbery when he saw the total, then realized the waiter had added Belle's and Corey's dinners to his bill. He peeled off fifty dollars in greenbacks and passed it over, thinking that paper money wasn't anywhere near as good as gold. This meal might equal half a week's pay, but Slocum had to look on it as an investment.

"Thank you, Mr. Slocum," Belle said, seeing that he had taken care of their bill, also. "Is it possible for you to begin immediately?"

"No reason I can't," he said slowly. He thought of finding a place to stay first. He still had almost a hundred dollars he'd won in the card game over at the Howling Wilderness. With the price of food so high, he knew that a hotel room would take a big bite out of his poke.

"Let's hurry," Belle said. "We have a meeting with Mr. Hearst in ten minutes." She stood quickly and Corey followed.

"Hearst? You mean George Hearst?" Slocum had heard of the San Francisco magnate. He owned a newspaper there run by his son William, and had often been rumored to be the richest man in California. Slocum doubted that claim since Crocker and Stanford and Sutro were so well heeled.

"He is interested in two of our properties," Belle said. "If they work out for him, perhaps the others might go for a decent price, too."

Slocum followed the two hurrying ladies through the gathering dusk, impressed at the company they kept. They stopped outside a large brick building with impressive gold lettering on its windows. Hearst didn't seem to be a man to keep his light under a bucket. His name was twice the size of the rest of the lettering.

"We are right on time," Belle said, pulling a large pocket watch from her purse and opening it. She studied its face for a moment, then snapped the case closed and looked up. Slocum opened the door for her and her sister. Corey graced him with a smile as she rushed past into the cigar-smoke-filled room.

A secretary looked up at the women, then glanced nervously into an inner office from which the blue billows of smoke emanated. He pushed to his feet and asked, "Is Mr. Hearst expecting you ladies?"

"Why, yes, of course he is," Belle said, acting as if this were the wittiest thing she'd ever heard. "We wish to talk about our daddy's silver mines."

"Watkins!" bellowed the walrus of a man in the office. "Are those the Flowers sisters?"

Corey and Belle both nodded and smiled shyly. Slocum stood back and watched, saying nothing. Belle was nothing like this and Corey had changed, too. The two women almost melted when Hearst pushed his way out to greet them. He puffed hard on a thick cigar, and his girth was more than any two men ought to carry, but Slocum felt the power that money lent radiating from the man. It wasn't hard to believe he was the wealthiest man in San Francisco—or the Comstock Lode.

"Well, ladies, come right on in. Have a seat. I'll be right with you." Hearst ignored Slocum as he turned to give his secretary instructions on titles and payment schedules. Not knowing what to do, Slocum followed Belle and Corey into the office. They were already seated in the room's only chairs other than Hearst's behind the massive polished wood desk. Slocum stood to one side where he wouldn't be in the way. He wanted to be able to see both the Flowers sisters and Hearst as they negotiated.

Hearst bustled back in and sat heavily in his chair. "I don't have much time, Miss Flowers. You wish to sell two of your late father's properties?"

"Why, yes, I believe we do," said Belle, looking at Corey as if she needed her sister's support. "We really don't know much about such things."

"They're not difficult," Hearst said, puffing on his cigar so hard he vanished in a momentary cloud of smoke. "The price you ask is out of the question. For a lesser amount, say two hundred thousand dollars, we can finish the deal."

"Oh, my goodness, what are we going to do?" wailed Belle, dabbing her eyes as if tears were forming. Slocum saw no reflection from moisture on her cheeks as she pretended to be distraught. "We need at least twice that to pay our daddy's debts. He seems to have not paid *any*thing in the last few months."

"Half a million is out of the question," Hearst said gruffly.

Corey began to cry and Belle held her. "There, there, Coreopsis, we'll find a way to pay those bills. I just know it."

"I'd need the assay reports and a fresh sample to be sure the mines aren't overworked. And the rest of the deed." Hearst rocked back and folded his hands on his rotund belly, looking satisfied at the deal he was making.

"The rest?" asked Belle. Slocum saw a flash of fear in her eyes that vanished as quickly as it appeared. "Whatever do you mean?"

"This is only the first page of the claim. Get a copy from the clerk tomorrow and have it on my desk by noon. We'll see to examining the properties the next day. And after my agents have looked the mines over, I'll have a check for three hundred thousand ready for you, when all's in order."

"Four hundred thousand in gold?" Belle asked timidly.

"Three-fifty in scrip and not one cent more, not even if it's the mother lode itself. I do declare, you ladies are worse thieves than Old Pancake Comstock himself."

"But he stole his claim from Allen and Hosea Grosch, sir," said Belle. "We are not stealing anything. Somehow, I have the feeling *you* are the one getting the better in this deal." She looked at him, then averted her eyes before he broke out in hearty laughter.

"Been nice talking to you ladies. If you'll excuse me, I have to discuss the matter of all that boiling water in the bottoms of my mines. Sutro thinks he can drain it, but it's going to cost too damned much for my liking."

"I assure you, Mr. Hearst, there is no water in our mines," Corey said solemnly. This set Hearst off on another gale of laughter. Belle took her sister's arm and almost dragged her from the office. Slocum followed silently, wondering at a deal for so much money. A hundred a week hardly seemed adequate to protect mines worth half a million dollars from claim jumpers.

But then Belle had broadly hinted there might be a bonus for his loyalty. Slocum couldn't keep his daydreams from rising up once more. On the street, under the pale yellow light cast by the gaslights, Belle stopped and fumbled in her purse. She pulled out a tattered piece of paper.

"Here is a map to the mines Mr. Hearst was so kind to buy. Please go check to see if all is right with them."

Slocum took the map and peered at it in the flickering light. It took a few seconds for him to orient the map with Virginia City. He tucked it in his pocket.

"Don't reckon there'll be any trouble. What can any claim jumper do overnight?" he asked.

"Never underestimate your enemies," Belle said seriously. Corey had to laugh at that, and Slocum wondered why. "You run on now, Mr. Slocum, and be back here by noon tomorrow. We need to complete our transaction with Mr. Hearst and need to know all is in order."

"See you then," Slocum said, realizing he would be riding most of the night checking the two mines. The Washoe Zephyr was beginning to blow and promised a night of gale-force wind. Still, he couldn't complain too much. Hearing that the Flowers sisters were closing a three-hundred-fifty-thousand-dollar deal with the likes of George Hearst assured Slocum of getting his pay.

Still . . .

Something didn't set well with him. He went to the Howling Wilderness and got on his horse, but he didn't turn the gelding's face toward the fabulous silver mines. The protesting horse walked slowly back toward Hearst's office. By the time Slocum had retraced his path, he saw Belle and Corey hurrying down C Street and making a quick turn at the next corner. Riding slowly, he watched and his curiosity began to get the better of him.

They weren't returning home—and he had assumed the ladies would at least ask him to escort them to their door. Virginia City was a rough and tumble town. A drunk miner, seeing such feminine beauty, might not be able to restrain his animal urges.

Slocum wondered at his own reasons for following them. Corey was lovely and Belle was gorgeous. Either of them could give a man a great deal of pleasure.

"Just seeing them home safely," he said to his horse. The animal turned and glared at him, as if wondering why Slocum couldn't do it on foot. Slocum urged the horse down the street to the alley where Belle and Corey had vanished.

Slocum kept riding, then dismounted and walked back. The women knelt by a door, intent on a lock. They whispered back and forth but he couldn't make out their words. He started down the alley to see if he could help when Corey let out a whoop of triumph. Belle hushed her, and they vanished into the darkened room beyond.

More curious than ever, Slocum walked to the door and peered inside. The two women had a large ledger out on a table and worked diligently on it. Glancing around, Slocum knew they had broken into the Virginia City land office. He watched them work for fifteen minutes, then slipped back to the street and mounted.

"Wonder what they're up to?" Slocum asked. The only answer he got was a loud neigh. He shook his head and rode out of town, hat pulled down to protect his face from the increasingly fierce wind, intent on following Belle's map to the first mine.

3

Slocum's face burned from the constant onslaught of the Washoe Zephyr. He had arrived at the first mine, the Silver Canary, around midnight and had entered carefully. Evidence of recent work on the mine showed that some ore was being taken. Slocum had taken a few chunks of quartz from deep in the mine and examined them by a small campfire.

Silver gleamed in the guttering light and assured him the Silver Canary's song was one of wealth.

Eating a brief meal of canned peaches, he laid back on his bedroll and caught a few hours sleep. He saw no reason to venture out into the fierce wind just to satisfy the unfounded worries of a woman convinced everyone in Virginia City was a thief. Nothing even hinted at claim jumpers visiting this mine.

The wind whining like a banshee through the rocks woke Slocum an hour before sunup. He stretched and brushed the dust from his face. His horse had fared a little better, being tethered on the lee side of a large boulder. He considered a quick breakfast, then decided the peaches he'd eaten hours earlier would hold him until he got back to Virginia City and a real meal. His mouth watered at the memory of his dinner steak the day before.

Getting his gear together, he saddled his horse and started for the second mine. The sooner he visited it, the sooner he could get back to report to the Flowers sisters.

Just past sunup, he saw a broken sign pointing the way to the Spit Bucket Mine. Slocum shook his head, wondering where the miners got their names. This claim hardly sounded worth the effort, yet he knew Hearst was willing to pay an incredible sum for both mines. From his brief check of the Silver Canary, it was valuable, but nowhere near worth three-hundred-fifty-thousand dollars. That meant the Spit Bucket had high-grade ore buried under its dilapidated sign.

Slocum lifted his leg and cocked it around the pommel, sitting and staring at the mine. A shack a ways down the hill was ready to fall over come the next strong gust, and the ore cart tracks leading into the mine were too rusty for use. The Spit Bucket needed considerable work to make it operational.

Swinging out of the saddle, Slocum walked to the mouth of the mine. He froze when the ominous sound of a gun cocking echoed from the shaft.

"You take another step and I'll blow your damned head off your shoulders," came the warning.

Slocum couldn't see anyone inside, but the crunch of boots against gravel told him his trouble lay inside the mine. He shifted weight, moving to one side.

"You get on that there horse and ride out, mister. I don't want no trouble, but I'll kill to keep my claim."

"This mine belongs to the Flowers family," Slocum said.

"Like hell it does!" A wizened old prospector crept out of the mine's mouth, a Damascus barrel shotgun preceding him. He waved the scattergun around like a magic wand. Slocum would have willingly disappeared except he worried he might be shot in the back. The old man didn't look to have an ounce of charity in his hunched-over body.

"There are deeds," Slocum started. He didn't want to mention the sale to George Hearst.

"Claim jumpers! That's what those . . . those—" The prospector began sputtering, unable to come up with a curse vile enough.

He hefted the shotgun to his shoulder and peered down the long barrel. Slocum saw the miner's finger tensing on the double triggers. He took another sidestep, forcing the man out of the mine if he wanted to keep Slocum covered.

"We can talk this over," Slocum said. A quick glance down showed him he still had the leather thong looped over the hammer of his Colt. It'd take him too long dragging out his six-shooter if shooting started. Jawboning his way past the old man looked to be his only chance.

"There's nothing to talk over. I don't want nothing to do with the damned Flowers family. Thieves, the lot of them. And Dalton's not the worst. That kid of his is . . ." The miner started sputtering again.

"Who's that?" Slocum asked. Belle was a sharp operator, but it didn't sound as if this grizzled prospector meant her or Corey.

"You know who. You're one of them. You're all out to steal my claim. I won't let you!"

Slocum dived for cover when he saw the way the man's shoulders tensed just prior to squeezing the triggers on the double-barreled shotgun. The loud roar deafened him and the foot-long tongues of flame momentarily blinded him. But Slocum felt only a few pellets rake his arm. Most of the deadly load had blown a limb off a juniper a few paces behind him.

Hitting the ground hard, Slocum started rolling. Both barrels had discharged. He wasn't sure if the old man wanted to be sure he was buzzard bait or if it had been an accident. Whatever the reason, it forced the prospector to break open the shotgun and reload. This gave Slocum the chance to slip the thong off his Colt Navy and draw.

"I don't want to shoot," he said, coming to his knees and aiming. At this range, he could hardly miss.

"Damned backshooting, bushwhackin' claim jumper!" The prospector discharged his shotgun again, this time into the ground at his feet. A cloud of dust rose, hiding him for a few seconds. By the time the air cleared, he had ducked back into the mine.

Slocum wasn't sure what he ought to do. He had no call going after the miner, but he had promised Belle to keep out any claim jumpers. That the old geezer thought of the Spit Bucket as his mine meant nothing. George Hearst wouldn't want any tangled claims, and all the Flowers sisters wanted was to dispose of their father's legacy. Slocum heaved a sigh and got to his feet.

He knew what had to be done, and he didn't relish it.

Moving slowly, he advanced until his left side pressed into the cold rock of the mine's entrance. He peered into the inky darkness. The miner hadn't bothered with a carbide light. Slocum knew he could send bullets ricocheting down the shaft and probably spook—or wound—the old man.

Slocum jumped a foot when another double load of buckshot ripped out of the mine, intent on his flesh. One pellet tore a hole through the brim of his hat.

"Enough of this," Slocum shouted. "This isn't your claim. Put down the scattergun, and I'll let you ride out just like nothing happened."

"The only thing that's gonna happen is me runnin' you off my claim!" The statement was punctuated with more buckshot. Splinters from the wood supports grazed Slocum's face. A small trickle of blood running down his cheek angered him more than it injured him.

"You can't stay in there forever," he said.

"Just you wait and see, you stinking, mangy coyote!" The old man started shooting again.

Slocum considered all the things he might do, but none struck his fancy. He finally called out, "I'm leaving. Don't go doing any more shooting. You've won." Slocum decided the Virginia City sheriff could come out and serve process on the man to get him from the mine. There wasn't any cause for anyone to lose a life over a hole in the ground, even if it was a rich claim.

Backing away, Slocum kept a sharp eye on the mouth of the mine. A dozen yards down the hill, he holstered his six-shooter and turned to his horse. The sixth sense that had kept him alive through the war and since saved him again. Slocum drew, turned, and crouched down just as another shotgun blast ripped at the air where his head had been. Two heavy pellets staggered him, but that didn't affect his aim.

The Colt fired straight and true. The prospector jerked upright and took a faltering step before sinking to his knees. He shouted incoherent curses—and Slocum saw he wasn't going to give up because of a bullet in his gut. The miner worried out two more shotgun shells from his pocket, struggling to chamber them.

Wounds burning as if liquid fire had been poured over his arm, Slocum stood to get a better shot. The prospector saw this and scuttled into the mine again, retreating like a stepped-on crab.

Slocum would have left this to the sheriff. Not now. The old man had tried to backshoot him—and there was more. He had drilled the prospector dead center. The man had a chunk of lead in the middle of his belly. It didn't kill him outright but it would sooner or later. Slocum wouldn't leave a wounded animal to die. He wasn't about to just ride off and let the man die, no matter how cantankerous and dangerous he was.

He approached carefully, his six-gun centered on the mouth of the mine. Tiny moans came from the shaft, but Slocum knew this might be a trick to lure him closer.

"Come on out, and I'll get you to a sawbones in Virginia City," he called.

"Claim jumper!" shrieked the miner. "You ain't takin' what's mine by law! I got a right to protect it from your kind. You and them Flowers—"

Slocum wasn't sure what happened to cut off the prospector's tirade. It might be a trap, but he didn't think so. He moved closer, dropped to a crouch, and peered around the timber supporting the mine's opening. A small lantern cast a shaky light on the dusty floor not twenty feet inside the mine. Of the miner he saw no trace.

Taking time to reload also gave him a chance to just listen. Timbers creaked deep inside the mine, but there wasn't any other sound. He took a deep breath, spun inside, and pressed hard against the wall to keep from silhouetting himself against the morning sky.

The quick move saved his life. Another shotgun blast tore past. Slocum wasn't touched this time since the lead was aimed too high and ripped out rock over his head. Once the cascade of dust stopped, Slocum moved deeper into the mine, cursing himself for a fool. He ought to just seal the mouth and let Hearst buy a grave.

A moan kept him moving. The old man wasn't good enough an actor to make that sound of pain and suffering. Slocum ducked into a side tunnel and waited. The carbide lamp was on the floor a pace away. He had to pass it if he wanted to find the old man.

Slocum worried over all the things he ought to do. If he went by the lamp, he'd be outlined by the light and a perfect target. There had to be another way. He looked around and found a length of roofing timber that had splintered. Taking the end, he pushed it out of the tunnel mouth until it poked against the carbide lamp.

Water inside sloshed a mite, and then the lamp moved away slowly. Slocum kept his distance and pushed slowly, moving the light ahead of him. He had to take the risk that there wasn't enough light cast on him for the old man to shoot.

"Stay away," came the weak command. "I'll kill you!"

"You need a doctor," Slocum said, keeping up his slow advance. He heard the shotgun's hammers cocking again. Falling flat, he waited for the roar and the hot passage of deadly lead pellets.

They never came.

Slocum moved faster now and saw the prospector's boot at the edge of the lamp's circle of illumination. He shoved hard on the lamp, turning it over and letting it roll deeper into the mine. The light came to rest against the far wall of the mine.

The miner sat on the floor, shotgun across his lap. From the way his head lolled to one side, Slocum knew the old fool had gone too far in trying to steal this claim.

Slocum kicked the shotgun away—and saw that the miner had run out of shells. The hammers had cocked over empty chambers. Snorting in disgust, Slocum holstered his Colt and hefted the old man's surprisingly frail body over his shoulders. It might be more than he deserved, but he would get a decent burial.

Stumbling and staggering down the hill to the shack, Slocum found a pick and a shovel. It took the better part of an hour to dig in the rocky soil, but he got a grave cut. He found a blanket in the shack, and a few pitiful belongings. Slocum wrapped the old man in the blanket and took the rest to the grave site.

Slocum rolled the prospector into the grave and tossed his belongings after him. On impulse, Slocum went through the man's papers.

"I hope God's more forgiving than I am, Obadiah Clark," said Slocum. He didn't cotton to any man opening up on him when his back was turned. He started to toss the rest of the papers into the grave when one caught his eye.

Slocum scratched his head as he read through what looked to be a deed for the Spit Bucket Mine. If it was a forgery, it was a damned good one. From all Slocum had seen of Obadiah Clark, he wasn't the kind to spend— or even have—money for a fake deed.

Slocum tucked the papers into his pocket, then set to work shoveling the thin, rocky soil over the man's body.

It was just past sunset when Slocum rode back into Virginia City. He had ridden all day, not pressing his tired gelding, and had been thinking hard about the papers in his pocket. Obadiah Clark might have bought the Spit Bucket Mine from some confidence man intent on bilking gullible miners out of what little money they had. Any con man worth his salt would have official-looking deeds.

How hard would it be to steal a handful when the land clerk was looking the other way? Slocum had heard of more intricate ways of stealing than this.

Still, it rankled like a burr under his saddle blanket the way Clark had fought so hard. He knew the Flowers family. The way he tried to find the proper descriptions for them every time he mentioned the mine told Slocum that Clark might have known them well. Or at least Dalton Flowers.

The Howling Wilderness was filled and the drunks were already spilling into the street. Slocum avoided them and any of the other saloons. The Melodian had drawn a huge crowd, and Virginia City seemed more boisterous than ever.

Slocum rode aimlessly through the streets—or so he thought until he found himself stopped outside the land office and just staring at the brick fronted building. What answers were locked up inside the ledgers? And did he really want to find out the truth?

Dismounting and tethering his horse at a nearby trough, he paced back and forth on the boardwalk until he reached his decision. The deed in his pocket seemed to burn hotter than the desert sun. The only way of putting that fire out was the water of truth.

Slocum ducked into the alley behind the land office where he had seen Belle and Corey the night before. He went to the door and examined it. Anyone checking for a break-in would have noticed the bright scratches on the lock. But who would check if nothing was missing inside?

Whipping out his knife, Slocum wedged it between door and lock. A few twists got the wood to give way. Some shaking and pounding sprung the latch and let him in. Slocum glanced back down the alley to be sure no one had heard him. The sheriff and any deputies would be patrolling farther down C Street, trying to keep the drunks from burning Virginia City to the ground again. And who cared about anyone jimmying a door to a land office?

He looked around the small office and shook his head. No cash, no gold stored here—that would be at the assay office next door. The only things of value were the fixtures, and lamps and chairs weren't the kind of treasure most thieves in a boomtown would want.

Slocum pulled a lamp closer and lit it with a lucifer, keeping the wick turned down low. He went to the huge bookcase against the side wall and studied the spines. Most of the writing was smudged, but he finally found a volume marked with the first two numbers of the registration on the deed in his pocket. He took it to a table and dropped it down with a loud bang.

It was at this very table he had seen Belle and Corey working on a book similar to the one he now opened. Slocum flipped through the pages quickly and came to a match with Clark's deed number.

The Spit Bucket was registered in the name of Dalton Flowers—and the ink was still damp.

4

Slocum put the records book back on the shelf and quickly left. He closed the door and decided no one would notice his tinkering. The wood was broken in two places but wedged back into place with a little work. The paint was cracked and peeling on the rest of the frame and only real effort would find where he—or the Flowers sisters—had broken into the land office.

He got his horse and walked it slowly to a stable he had seen down on Peach Street, thinking hard about what to do after seeing the gelding fed and brushed down. Belle and Corey were involved in something more than selling their father's silver mines, but Slocum wasn't sure what it might be. Obadiah Clark was sure they were claim jumpers, but Slocum wasn't convinced. Not yet.

The long, fine auburn hair trailing back from Belle's pale oval face as she turned and let the wind whip it like a war banner kept coming back to Slocum's mind. And Corey. She was as lovely, but it was Belle who drew Slocum like a loadstone pulls iron nails.

Belle had a quick mind and fine sense of humor. Corey seemed less intelligent but perhaps more inclined to enjoy herself. The more Slocum thought of the sisters, the less sure he was of anything about them. Could either of them have stolen the Spit Bucket Mine from Clark? They had a productive mine in the Silver Canary, and from what Belle said, these two weren't the only ones they owned now that their father had passed on.

They were just two that George Hearst wanted to buy for a fabulous amount. How many more mines did the sisters own?

Still, Slocum didn't like the notion that Obadiah Clark was positive *he* was being robbed. And the still-wet ink in the land office told of some dirty dealing.

Slocum went into the Howling Wilderness and looked around. No card games for him tonight. The green felt tables had been pushed to one side to accommodate a small ring for cock fighting. Feathers flew and the fighting roosters squawked so loud they sometimes drowned out the drunken cheers of the miners betting on them. Slocum took a whiskey and nursed it, still not sure what he should do.

The din around him faded as he lost himself in considering the best route out of Virginia City. He couldn't discount the possibility that Belle had sent him around to the mines to kill Obadiah Clark, and this after saying straight out all she wanted was someone to keep the mines from the hands of claim jumpers.

It hadn't occurred to Slocum that she was getting him involved in doing the very thing she said she wanted to prevent.

He knocked back the whiskey and let it puddle in his belly. The warmth spread, and he knew he ought to leave town. And yet his feet turned toward the saloon door so he could look uphill toward the fine mansions on Gold Hill. Belle and Corey were up there somewhere. He wondered why he hadn't bothered asking which house was theirs.

Slocum smiled ruefully. He remembered why. He had been intent on escorting them back to their home and they had taken a side trip—through the land office records. He knew now what they'd been up to.

Or did he? How could he know what the two sisters had done once inside the office? He assumed they had forged their claim to the Spit Bucket Mine. Their business in the office might not have had anything to do with that claim. They might have been there for some other reason.

Slocum shook his head. He was grasping at straws. Who stood to gain if Obadiah Clark wasn't the legitimate owner of the Spit Bucket? Always ask who profited, he told himself, and he'd never go far astray.

"You gonna stand there all night?" asked a miner behind him. "I got other dives to drink dry, and time's a'wastin'!"

"You know where the Flowers mansion is?" Slocum asked suddenly. He had to talk to Belle one last time before he left Virginia City. He wanted to hear her tell him the truth.

"Flowers? Heard tell of a Dalton Flowers but don't rightly know where he's holed up." The miner pushed past, on his way to another night of debauchery. Slocum almost called after him, asking to join him on his rounds. But he held back. It couldn't be too hard finding Belle and Corey. Such lovely women in a boom town would draw attention wherever they went.

He started walking, heading up past B Street toward Gold Hill. The mansions looked like dark hulking beasts now, removed from the glare of the gaslights in the streets. Inner lighting turned windows into eyes and doors into gaping mouths in the huge houses. He had just begun walking down the street when a deputy stopped him.

"Where you headin'?" the deputy demanded, hand resting on his six-shooter.

"I'm looking for the Flowers house," Slocum said. "Belle Flowers hired me yesterday to look after some of her property."

"Belle Flowers?" The deputy scratched his chin, then looked Slocum over. "That's Dalton Flowers's older daughter, ain't it?"

"It is. And Coreopsis is the younger," Slocum supplied, figuring this might influence the deputy into letting him walk along the street where the riches of Virginia City came to rest.

"Don't know of her. Just Belle and that good-for-nothing son of Dalton Flowers's."

Slocum didn't recollect Belle ever mentioning a brother. If she had one, why hadn't she sent him out to look after their inheritance? This made Slocum all the more eager to find Belle. He hated to leave a town with so many questions begging for answers. And there was the matter of his money. He felt he had earned the hundred dollars in gold she had promised him.

He had left Obadiah Clark dead, and Slocum hated to be used as a hired gun. When he killed, he did it for his own reasons, not someone else's. Even when that someone was as lovely as Belle Flowers.

"How come you don't know where your employer lives?" the deputy asked, tilting his head to one side, as if this would let him see the truth better.

"They hired me and sent me out to their mine. I took longer getting back and missed meeting them at their business office." Slocum made a vague gesture toward C Street where most of the business in town was centered.

"I seen Belle Flowers goin' into a house the other day. Don't know that it's hers, though. That's it up yonder," the deputy said, coming to a decision about Slocum. "Don't go makin' any trouble. I'll be keepin' an eye peeled for you now."

"There won't be any trouble," Slocum said, wondering if he lied. If Belle paid him his blood money, that would end it and he'd move on. Or maybe some other opportunity in Virginia City might open for him. Getting the greenbacks folded in his shirt pocket had been easy enough. Drunk miners neither knew nor cared about odds at poker.

He trudged up the increasingly steep grade until he came to the front of the house the deputy had pointed out to him.

The gables were trimmed with wooden lace and two bay windows dominated the front of the imposing house. Lace curtains as white as snow were closed, but Slocum saw people moving in the front room. He opened the iron gate and started up the terraced steps, stopping when he got to the front door.

Slocum wondered if this was worth it. If the law found out he had killed Obadiah Clark, they might not see it as being self-defense the way he did. They might take it into their heads that Clark had the legitimate claim and Slocum was trying to do him out of his silver. All Slocum had to go on was Belle's word—and he was beginning to doubt that was worth a hill of beans.

He took a step forward and knocked hard on the door. The resonant echoing startled him. The night was quieter up here than he expected from the boisterous goings-on down the hill.

The door opened a crack and Belle peered out.

"Evening, Belle," he said. "Don't reckon you were expecting to see me."

The auburn-haired beauty opened the door, her eyes wide. "Why, whatever makes you say that, Mr. Slocum. Do come in. We wondered what happened to you. We'd told you to be back by noon. You are all right, aren't you?"

Slocum walked in and stopped, his footsteps echoing hollowly. Something about the emptiness of the house told him that the Flowers sisters intended a long trip away from Virginia City soon.

"This way, please," Belle said, gesturing toward the front room where Slocum had seen people moving behind the lace curtains. As he entered the parlor, Corey shot to her feet, her blue eyes wide and bright.

"Why, Belle, you didn't tell me he was coming this evening. I am quite surprised. Welcome, Mr. Slocum."

Slocum looked the room over, not sure what he was hunting. He shook his head. He had been on the trail too long, and his entire body ached. Just as he started to comment on it, Belle exclaimed, "Your arm! You've been wounded!"

"Obadiah Clark," he said, waiting for a reaction.

"Him," Corey said in disgust. "That old bushwhacker ought to be run out of the district. He can't go around shooting people. Belle, you go right now and summon the sheriff."

"Getting the sheriff isn't going to do anything," Slocum said. "Clark's not going to backshoot anyone else."

"No, John, you mean—" Belle's hand covered her mouth as if she were horrified. Her gestures told of fright but her eyes conveyed no such message. If anything, Slocum thought she was glad at the outcome. That only confirmed what he had suspected. She and Corey had picked him to eliminate a problem for them: Obadiah Clark.

"He made a good case for owning the Spit Bucket Mine," he said.

"He did not!" Belle stamped her foot hard in anger. "He and Papa were always feuding. They were partners once, but he tried to double-cross us. Papa cut him off at the knees!"

"Yes, John," cut in Corey. "Papa made sure he didn't keep a single property. That mine is ours!"

Slocum wished he could shake the feeling the two women were laughing at him. Their expressions said one thing but he had a gut feeling nothing he saw or heard was right. He started to mention the wet ink in the land office ledger when Belle brushed over his wounded arm. He winced as pain lanced into his shoulder.

"Go get a doctor, Corey," said Belle. "This is worse than it looked when he came in. See how the blood has matted the shirt to the arm?"

"I don't know where I can find one this time of night," Corey said doubtfully. "The only good doctor's likely to be out on a drunk. But I'll go look, if you like."

"Do," said Belle. "I'll get the wound cleaned and ready."

"That's not necessary," Slocum protested. He'd had worse wounds than this and never noticed. Clark's shotgun pellets had only grazed him. There wasn't any need for a doctor to start digging.

"And he is filthy from the trail," Belle said, looking at him with a hot look he couldn't mistake. "I want to take care of him."

"I'll be right back, Belle," said her sister. Corey smiled wickedly, then pulled her shawl around her shoulders and rushed from the house. The door slammed and echoed as if the place were mostly empty. Slocum glanced through the curtains and saw Corey hurrying toward town.

"Let me help, John," said Belle. She began peeling the shirt away from the caked blood. Slocum closed his eyes, took a deep breath, then gasped. Belle had finished taking his shirt off.

And her tongue was working all over his chest, drifting lower, toward his navel. He opened his eyes and saw the woman down on her knees. She fumbled a little getting his gun belt off, then worked with more assurance at the buttons holding up his pants. The thought flashed through his mind that she'd had lots of practice at this little chore.

Then all thought left him and only pleasure remained. Her hot mouth found a target and worked avidly on it. Slocum felt himself hardening. He put his hands down on the sides of the woman's head and guided her back and forth a bit faster. He stiffened under her oral onslaught, even as his knees turned to water.

"Do you like this, John?" Belle whispered.

"What man wouldn't?" he croaked out, his voice sticking in his throat.

"No *man* wouldn't," she said in a husky whisper. "And you are quite a man." Her mouth worked more on him while her hands worked his pants off. Slocum helped the best he could, kicking at his boots to get them free. Somehow Belle was a magician and made everything vanish with hardly any effort on his part.

"I don't want to soil my fine clothing," she said, moving away from him. She stood straight, shoulders back, breasts thrusting boldly against the soft fabric of her bodice. Belle began working at the buttons. Her blouse fell open to reveal twin peaks of the most succulent flesh Slocum had ever seen.

Her breasts stood poised and high on her chest, capped with lust-hard nipples. Belle swayed to and fro and worked her skirt down past her flaring hips. She lithely stepped from the pile of clothing at her ankles, as buck naked as Slocum.

"See anything you like?" she teased. Belle pirouetted around to give him a complete look at what she offered.

"Everything," he said honestly. Slocum might have seen a more beautiful woman, but for the life of him he couldn't remember when or where. Belle took away both memory and will. She dropped down again, her long fingers stroking up and down his legs, dancing over his buttocks, moving around and teasing his balls.

When she squeezed down hard, Slocum gasped and thought he was going to be ruined for life. But before the pain could register fully, it was replaced with such pleasure that he felt faint. Belle's lips worked over the tip of his manhood, licking and lapping, roughly tormenting him, then lightly sampling as if she had a feather instead of a tongue.

"I'm ready for you, John. Are you ready for me?" Belle rose and straddled him, then sank down, her nether lips parting as she worked ever lower. Slocum watched in fascination as the tip of his stiffened organ vanished into the woman's humid interior. Belle sank down fully, sitting on his lap and looking into his green eyes. Her brown eyes glowed with lust.

Slocum had let her have her way this far. It was his turn to return some of the delight she was giving him. His hands cupped her breasts and squeezed gently. When he caught the coppery tips between thumbs and forefingers, he started squeezing and turning. Belle's expression changed to one of complete lust.

"Like that?" Slocum asked, knowing the answer.

"Yes, damn you, yes, yes," Belle hissed. "How do you like this?"

Slocum wasn't sure what she did. It felt as if a hand encased in velvet had gripped at his length and squeezed powerfully. As suddenly as it had started, the pressure slackened, then returned, milking him for all he was worth. Slocum couldn't keep still any longer. The urges mounting in his loins demanded action, movement, burying himself as far into Belle as he could get.

He lifted off the floor and drove his hips upward, spearing her even more deeply. He kept up the movement with his hands and felt her heart throbbing with desire through the taut nipples on each breast. Twisting just a little gave him a different angle of entry into her heated interior. This set Belle off like a skyrocket.

She shrieked and moaned and thrashed about like a bronco not wanting to be saddle broke. Slocum rode her, catching the woman around her trim waist and carrying her over to the floor, reversing their positions. Firmly between her slender legs, Slocum began stroking now. He had to hurry because of the white-hot tide building in his balls.

But Belle shivered and shook like a leaf in a high wind, a hot flush rising up from her breasts to her shoulders and neck seconds before Slocum spilled his seed into her.

Her eyelids fluttered and a smile came to her lips. "You're quite a man, John, quite a man."

Slocum winced, his arm throbbing now from the activity he'd just enjoyed so much with Belle. A thin trickle of blood started from the shallow wounds.

"Bet even your arm feels better," Belle said, running her fingers along the heavily muscled shoulder and down toward the wound, as if to stroke it. Slocum pulled away.

"You owe me a hundred dollars," he said. Shock crossed Belle's face, then she understood. A slow smile crossed her face, and her eyes twinkled with mischief.

"Your week's pay. Of course."

"I want to be on my way." Even as the words left Slocum's lips, he damned himself for a fool. If he stayed, even for a few more days, he'd receive pay far beyond mere gold. It had been *good* with Belle, and he thought it might get better.

"One thousand dollars," she said unexpectedly. Her naked breasts bobbed as she spoke. Belle pushed up to her elbows and looked squarely into his green eyes. "In gold. For just one more day."

"One more day?" he asked.

"And night. One more night," Belle Flowers said, and Slocum couldn't refuse her or her money.

5

Slocum flexed his left arm and had to admit Belle had done a good job patching him up. She had finished washing out the shallow, bloody scratches and put iodine on them. By the time she finished with the last linen bandage, Corey returned. Slocum wondered where the blonde had been for so long.

"I couldn't find the doctor," she said brightly. From the way she said it, Slocum doubted she had even tried. She knew what her sister and Slocum had been up to. There was no way she couldn't know. Some of Belle's clothing was still scattered around the room, left there after she put on a long robe.

"Doesn't matter much," Slocum allowed. He stretched again, testing the limits of his movement. The muscles protested a mite but nothing he couldn't live with. And there was a warmth still burning inside him that more than countered any discomfort he might feel. Belle was one hell of a woman.

"Belle can be quite the nurse," Corey said, sitting on a chair where Belle's skirt was draped over the arm. She seemed to be oblivious to all evidence of her sister's love-making—but Slocum knew it was feigned. The woman's blue eyes fixed on him and burned with a lust matched only by Belle's.

They were quite a pair.

"John has agreed to go along with our little . . . game." Belle looked at him from half-lowered eyes.

"What game?" he asked, suddenly wary. She had offered him more money than he was likely to see in two years but hadn't told him what he had to do to earn it. Better sense returned now that the glow of their lovemaking was fading.

"Oh, poo, it's nothing," said Corey. "Belle did tell you about impersonating him, didn't she?"

"Him? Who am I supposed to impersonate?" Slocum wanted no part of this. He had killed in self-defense but the thought kept creeping back that Belle and Corey had set him up in some way. Obadiah Clark's deed rode in Slocum's pocket, and it might have been legitimate. He suspected the two women were capable of about anything since he suspected they had altered the land office records.

"Oh, John, no one in particular," Belle said, sitting beside him on the sofa. She crossed her legs in a very unladylike manner, her robe opening and showing naked thigh. Belle moved slightly and laid her hand on his arm. "All we want is for you to dress up real nice—"

"We have clothing upstairs," Corey cut in. "That is, if you don't mind wearing a dead man's clothes."

"What's going on? You're promising me a thousand dollars to pass myself off as a dead man?"

"No, not at all, John. Corey means they were our papa's clothes. You two were about the same size. All you need do is put on his fanciest clothes and tell the men we'll meet that you're a mining engineer."

"From South Dakota," Corey continued smoothly. "All these men will be from San Francisco. I doubt they would know many mining engineers from the Black Hills."

"I don't know enough to convince anyone I'm an engineer," Slocum protested.

Belle began stroking his arm gently, her fingernails digging in just enough to cause cold shivers to pass up and down his spine. "Why, John, don't you worry about that. They'll be distracted. All you need to do is look prosperous."

"And for that," Corey said, "you'll need a bath. I'll start some water heating. Belle can show you where the tub is." Corey left the room, the hitch in her walk capturing Slocum's attention until Belle touched him lightly on the cheek and turned him back.

"I can use a bath, too," she said. She took his hand and led him from the room, her robe falling open as she walked. Slocum trailed behind, wondering what the hell he had gotten himself into.

"There they are," said Belle Flowers, shielding her eyes with her fan. "Right on time. I like that in a man."

Slocum ran his finger under the tight celluloid collar. The fancy duds he wore were too tight across the shoulders, and he didn't dare squat down. The seat of his britches would tear open if he did. At least he hadn't embarrassed himself on the ride to the Silver Canary Mine since Belle had insisted he join them in her buggy. Sitting astride his gelding would have caused studs and seams to pop everywhere.

Worst of all, Slocum had left his Colt Navy back at the Flowers house. He felt damned near naked without its familiar weight on his left hip.

"Quit fidgeting, John," said Corey, enjoying his discomfort. "Look rich and like you're used to wearing those clothes." Her blue eyes danced as she gave him a once over. "I *do* so like the way everything fits. Especially your britches." She smiled wickedly and turned to greet the two men riding up. Corey had gone from lustful to demur in the wink of a long-lashed eye.

Not for the first time Slocum wondered why he had allowed himself to get tangled up in the scheme these two lovely ladies were weaving. The money was part of it—and being with Belle didn't hurt much, either. And if the auburn-haired beauty ever flagged, he guessed Corey would take her place in a flash. His mind wandered for a moment as he considered what it would be with both of them in his bed.

Then he had to meet George Hearst's men. He shook hands and mumbled greetings, but the two men hardly noticed him. They fell all over themselves with the ladies, Belle hooking her arm through one man's and Corey the other. Slocum had seen packs of dogs work the same way. They circled and singled out their prey, then moved in, depending on the rest of the pack for support.

Slocum wondered where he came into the picture—and that was another reason for staying a spell longer. The two women were up to something and he didn't know what it might be. Whatever it was, it promised huge returns. He'd already been promised a thousand dollars, eleven hundred if he counted the salary as their foreman.

All he had to do now was collect it.

"Oh, John, do tell these gentlemen about the mine. You know about ore grade and other dreary things." Belle batted her eyelashes at the man she clung to, the one who had introduced himself as Sam Hanrahan. Slocum could have told Hanrahan the mine was ten percent green cheese and not been heard. Still, he had to earn his money.

"This is picture ore," he said, entering the mine. "Blue dirt everywhere you look. Assay is high, maybe as much as ten ounces of silver per ton. Doesn't take much to get it out, and shipment to the mills over in Washoe Valley is easy."

He was right when he thought the men would ignore him. They took his samples and said nothing directly. They nodded and turned immediately to Belle and Corey. Slocum grew a little irritated, then forced himself to calm. This was a legitimate deal. The Silver Canary Mine belonged to the Flowers sisters, even if the Spit Bucket Mine might have been stolen through forgery.

"Good, good, it's everything you said it would be," Hanrahan said. "Let's get on over to the other mine, and we can be back in Virginia City for a little celebration before sundown."

"Why don't we just go on back to town now and start celebrating early?" suggested Corey. "John'll confirm that the other mine is as good as this one."

"Better," said Belle, snuggling closer to the man whose arm she clung to like a leech. "All this technical talk of assay and numbers and things makes my head spin." She pretended to be faint and let Hanrahan support her, his arm around her waist. "Let's do get on back to town."

Slocum saw the men consider a few extra hours with the Flowers sisters. Then he saw a touch of fear enter both men's eyes.

"Mr. Hearst wouldn't like it," said Hanrahan. "It won't take long, Miss Flowers. Your engineer knows his ore."

Belle gave Slocum a hot, bold look and said, "He knows about so many things. But let's do hurry. The sun is getting hot." She waved her fan rapidly like a butterfly's wings and disengaged from the man's arm, subtly showing her displeasure with him. Hearst's agent trotted after her like a lost puppy dog.

Slocum stood and watched for a moment, wondering if he was behaving any differently. He shook his head and trailed along, knowing he ought to get his money—in gold—and then ride on out of Virginia City. Things might get too hot for him soon.

He climbed into the buggy and took the reins. Belle smiled and waved to the men on their horses. Then she said to Slocum, "You're doing a fine job, John. There might be a . . . bonus in this for you tonight."

"Sounds as if you have a night already planned," he said.

"Why, John, you sound bitter. Don't be. This is just business. We need these mines sold to Mr. Hearst as soon as possible. Our financial condition is a bit shaky without the money." Corey Flowers shifted slightly in the buggy, her hand resting on Slocum's leg. It might have been accidental, but he didn't think so as she moved and brushed across his crotch. Both women knew how to sink their hook deep and reel in their catch.

"We'll ride on ahead and look it over, just to speed up the inspection," called Hanrahan, the agent that Slocum took to be in charge.

"Oh, wait, no!" exclaimed Belle. "Do ride along with us. It's so much more civilized. And these are dangerous roads."

"Not too dangerous," the other man said, riding beside the buggy.

"Mr. Slocum isn't armed, and neither are we," Corey said almost shyly. Slocum had heard some tall tales in his day. He'd pit either of these women against a timber rattler, and get odds on the bet. Corey and Belle might not be carrying pistols, but they were far from helpless.

"Did hear tell of some road agents working this stretch," Hanrahan called from behind the buggy. "Don't reckon it'd suit Mr. Hearst none if we let these fine ladies get held up."

Slocum guided the buggy along the rocky road, making better time getting to the Spit Bucket Mine than he had on horseback. He knew where he was going this time, and he wanted to get the inspection over. A fresh grave might draw a curious question or two. Without a six-shooter in his hand, Slocum wasn't sure how he would get out of answering who was buried under the rocks.

He need not have worried. He pulled the buggy up in front of the tumble-down shack, hoping the two agents wouldn't go poking around inside—or out back. The instant he reined back, both Belle and Corey were beckoning to Hearst's men to help them down.

"This way, gentlemen," Belle said, pointing the way up the slope to the mouth of the mine. "You will find that Mr. Slocum has checked it out completely. Do go on and tell them about the technical things you told me last night."

Slocum knew Belle was teasing him. He didn't let on. "The mine might prove as rich as the Silver Canary Mine, but—"

"But it might be even richer," Corey cut him off. She glared at him. "The assay is even higher. Why, my papa gave me this piece of ore just before he died. He told me, 'Coreopsis, honey, look at what I pulled out of that silly-named mine.' " She handed the chunk of ore to the man on her arm. "I don't know a solitary thing about mining. Is it really so very special, as my poor, departed papa hinted?"

Hearst's agent took the nugget and stared.

"Sam, look at this! This might be the damnedest, richest ore I ever saw. This is close to being a nugget of pure silver. Never seen anything like it before."

"That's my feeling," Slocum said, staring at the ore. It gleamed bright and shiny in the hot Nevada sunlight. Wherever Corey had gotten it, it wasn't out of the Spit Bucket Mine. All he had seen inside showed some low-grade ore, but nothing like this.

Slocum had never seen ore as rich as this silver nugget—ever.

"We'll just take a quick look inside," mumbled the man holding the nugget. "I want to see for myself."

"Is there any need?" asked Slocum, trying to head him off. Corey had overstepped the bounds of credulity. This was too rich a nugget for the engineer not to demand seeing the mother lode for himself. Such rich ore would let him scrape the silver out with his fingernails.

"Oh, Mr. Slocum, do let them look," said Belle. "We have nothing to hide." She looked sure of herself. Slocum wished for a six-shooter. And he cast a quick glance over his shoulder to the rear of the shack. To him the mounded rock of Obadiah Clark's grave looked like a beacon. So far, no one else had noticed.

He turned back when the two men emerged from the mine. He should have joined them, to steer them toward the richest veins of ore, such as they were. But the expressions on the men's faces told Slocum they were trying to conceal something.

"Everything looks in order, Miss Flowers," Hanrahan said. "Let's get on back to town and have Mr. Hearst sign the papers."

"Oh, good," sighed Corey. "This means we will receive our money?"

"The mine is everything you've said it was," the other man said. Again Slocum saw the men try to keep from smirking. The Spit Bucket wasn't that rich, and they ought to have laughed when they didn't find anything inside to match the fabulous nugget Corey had given them.

He wanted to look the mine over again, just to be sure.

"Mr. Slocum, please, let's get back to Virginia City," said Belle. The steel edge to her voice told him he wasn't going to be allowed the few minutes it would take to verify what Hearst's agents seemed to have discovered. She turned and looked steadily at Clark's grave, then back to Slocum. "Now, Mr. Slocum, let's start back *now*."

Slocum knew when he was being threatened, and he didn't like it one bit. But he saw that the others were already on the road back. He'd have to drive the horse pulling the buggy hard to match their pace. He climbed in, a woman on either side.

"Don't go asking questions that are of no concern, John," Belle warned. "And we won't take notice of that fresh grave behind the shack."

"Now, Belle, that's no way to talk to John," said Corey, hanging on his arm and rubbing against him like a cat greeting a friend. "He helped us convince those fine men what good properties we had to sell."

"The Silver Canary Mine is decent, but this one—" He looked over his shoulder, then shook his head. He just hadn't done enough hard looking at the mine, too bothered about killing Clark. If Hearst's agents were right, the Spit Bucket Mine might rival anything found in Six Mile Canyon or on Gold Hill. The Ophir mine had been gophered out until the top of Mount Davidson was falling off. This could be the new mother lode, and it might make George Hearst even wealthier than he was.

It could breathe fresh life into Virginia City and prolong the boom for years to come. It was more than a rich mine, it was the new lifeblood for an entire town.

Slocum rode back to Virginia City wondering how he could stake a claim and get in on the new rush.

"There you are, ladies," Slocum heard George Hearst saying. "My agents report that the mines are in good condition and worth the asking price."

"Oh, Mr. Hearst, they are worth far more than you are giving us, but we do want to return to San Francisco. This is such an uncivilized place," Belle said.

"It's not so bad. The opera house has scheduled Edwin Booth for a performance of the bard's *Macbeth*. Virginia City has its finer points."

"I am sure, but we do prefer San Francisco," Corey said. "And your generosity will make it all the more attractive for us now."

Slocum saw Corey putting stacks of greenbacks into her purse. When the small clutch purse was filled, Belle came over and pushed the rest of the money into hers.

"You ladies want my men to go with you to the bank? I don't think there'd be any trouble, but that is a considerable amount of money to be carrying, even in broad daylight."

"That's kind of you to offer, Mr. Hearst, but our foreman is outside. He'll take good care of us," said Belle. She shook Hearst's hand, then waited impatiently for Corey to do likewise. Then they hurried from the mining magnate's office to join Slocum.

"Let's go, John," Belle said under her breath. "I really do not like that man."

On the street, Belle and Corey stopped, then smiled broadly. "We did it, sister," Corey said. "We sold the mines."

"You go on," Belle told her. "Keep them busy for a few minutes. I'll be right along."

Slocum saw Hearst's two agents step out from the café where he had met the Flowers sisters. Corey guided both men back inside. It was apparent Belle and Corey were going to celebrate with the men they had just met.

"Don't reckon you need my services anymore," Slocum said. "You owe me for pretending to be your engineer. And the hundred for a week's work as your foreman."

"Why, John, the week's not over yet." Belle reached into her purse and counted out a thousand dollars in greenbacks. She handed it over. He quickly folded the bills and tucked it into his vest pocket. It never paid showing this much money, especially in a wide-open town like Virginia City.

"Keep the hundred, then," Slocum said.

"John, you do me wrong. Here." Belle handed him a hundred-dollar bill from her stash. "But I do wish you would stay, just a while longer."

"Why? You've sold the mines your father left."

"We've sold two of them. We have other properties. It won't take a week. Please stay." She looked up, her brown eyes promising the delights that could be his.

"I've got places to go," he said, resisting her charms.

"Another thousand dollars by Saturday," she whispered. "And a bonus." Belle's fingers lingered on his arm, then tightened and pulled him closer. She gave him a quick, unladylike kiss. "You'll like it. I promise."

"Saturday?" he asked.

"Come up to the house at midnight. We can discuss your duties further," Belle Flowers said. She grinned her wicked grin and spun, bustling off down the street to the café. Slocum wasn't sure what he was getting himself into, but he was enjoying it so far.

6

The money burned a hole in Slocum's pocket. He'd never had so much before, even if it was in scrip rather than the solid gold coin Belle had promised when he accepted her job offer. Somewhere around eleven o'clock, he found himself buying drinks for everyone in the Howling Wilderness Saloon, and he wasn't sure exactly why except that he had money. After knocking back some fiery liquor that the barkeep told him was Kentucky whiskey and which had never been within a thousand miles of that fine bourbon-producing state, Slocum backed off and just watched the boisterous crowd.

Again he got the feeling of intense desperation among the miners. The days of the Ophir and the Savage and the Virginia and Yellow Jacket and Chollar-Potosi were in Virginia City's past. These men knew it and tried to hold back the dark tides of depression by pretending to be prosperous and hopeful. For a few minutes Slocum had joined them because he knew something they didn't.

The Spit Bucket Mine might just put Virginia City back on the map and trigger a new boom. And George Hearst was sitting in the catbird seat with the deeds to the Flowers sisters' two mines.

A darker mood settled over Slocum. He sank down to an empty table and nursed what was left in his shot glass. Men passed him, some bumping into his sore arm, but he ignored them. Belle was playing a dangerous game if the two mines weren't exactly as she represented. But Slocum had no reason to think the mines weren't her legacy—except for the body of Obadiah Clark moldering in a new grave.

Boom? Bust? One of those futures awaited the men in the room. Slocum took out his brother Robert's watch and flipped open the case. Belle had said to come up to the house at midnight. Slocum had almost a half hour before the hands crossed. He snapped it shut, wondering if he ought to go. He was rich now. Greed kept him on the hook as surely as Belle's body.

Slocum smiled crookedly. Those weren't the only two reasons he was staying around. His curiosity would kill him deader than a doornail one day, but he had to find out what was going on. He had watched two consummate actresses this afternoon working their audience. Hearst's agents had overlooked the obvious and seen only what Belle and Corey wanted them to see.

But that silver nugget!

Slocum shook the fog from his brain. Too many questions and not enough answers.

He checked the watch one last time and went outside into the cold night air. The sudden shock of walking into the Washoe Zephyr blowing hard down the street wiped out any intention Slocum had of going to the Flowers house. He shouldn't let Belle call all the shots. Slocum had money riding in his pocket. He turned toward the largest building in Virginia City, the International Hotel.

Five stories tall and made of red brick, it had bright gaslights in front of it and looked to be the final word in elegance. He'd never seen anything in St. Louis or San Francisco to match it. Slocum crossed the dusty street and walked briskly, the harsh wind at his back. Entering the huge lobby, Slocum stopped and just stared. He knew he had to spend some of his money staying here.

At the far end of the luxurious lobby stood an open elevator cage with a liveried boy inside to run it. Slocum had heard of elevators but had never ridden in one. If for no other reason, he had to stay here to ride up the full five floors in this miracle of science. He registered at the marble front desk, paid in advance, and made the elevator boy run him up and down to his room on the third floor a half-dozen times before he was content.

In the palatial room bigger than some barns he had seen, he slept peacefully between crisp white linen sheets in a feather bed. He could get real used to such luxury. And the money Belle had paid him for the impersonation.

Slocum ate breakfast at the International's café, looking at the wad of bills he still had left after paying a hundred dollars for the room and twenty for the food. Rested, satisfied, Slocum went outside. He had never stayed in such a hotel before, and he wasn't likely to any time soon again. The prices were too steep for his liking, but he had always wondered how men like Hearst and Crocker and Sutro lived. The taste appealed to him.

He wondered if Belle was angry that he had not shown up last night—or if she even noticed he had slipped the invisible leash she tried to put around his neck. She and Corey had been well occupied with Hearst's two mining agents, probably all night long. Slocum had no idea what devilment the two women were cooking up, but Hearst's two assistants looked to be at the heart of it.

Another mine sale might mean even more money riding high in Slocum's vest pocket. He stretched again, felt seams in his fancy duds begin to give, and considered buying some of his own that would fit. Slocum shook off the notion. Why spend money on clothes he wouldn't wear more than once or twice? He wasn't some fancy-ass engineer from the

Dakotas. He was John Slocum, a man with wanted posters on him circulating throughout the West.

He looked around the town and on impulse headed for the land office. Slocum stopped and peered in through the front window and saw a clerk hunched over his ledgers. Slocum went in. The bespectacled clerk didn't bother looking up.

Slocum checked to be sure the man wasn't working on the ledger the Flowers sisters had altered. A new volume was spread under the clerk's steel-nibbed pen. Slocum let out a little sigh of relief, then knew what he had to ask.

"I need to check a deed," he said. Only then did the clerk look up. The man pushed bifocals up his nose and peered at Slocum.

"Maybe I can help, maybe I can't. What do you have in mind?"

Slocum pulled Obadiah Clark's deed from his pocket, smoothed it, and passed it across to the clerk. The man adjusted his glasses again before studying it.

"Yep."

"What's that mean?" Slocum asked, looking hard at the man for some clue. "Is this deed legitimate?"

"That's my signature at the bottom. Can't say I remember signing this specific deed, but then old Obie Clark brought in hundreds of claims. Sometimes, he'd bring in a dozen at a time. A body gets tired after a while taking care of such nonsense."

"You knew—know—Obadiah Clark?"

"You buy this off him? That old codger's always trying to sell off his worthless claims." The land clerk studied Slocum as if he were the world's prize fool.

"This one's no good?" Slocum frowned.

"Didn't say the deed was worthless. Claim's as right as rain. Can't pass judgment on the quality of the ore on the land. What's this to you, anyway?"

Slocum dodged the question and asked another. "How long has Clark been partners with Dalton Flowers? I understand they own a good deal in common."

The clerk looked shocked for a moment, then laughed uproariously. He took off his glasses and wiped tears from his eyes. "Excuse me, mister, but that's about the funniest thing I ever heard. Obie and Flowers were anything *but* partners. Always at each other's throats, they were, up till the day Flowers died. I do declare, they spent all their time callin' each other names."

"Like claim jumpers?" asked Slocum.

"That was the least of what they called each other," the clerk allowed. "Can't ever see them as partners." The man looked around as if someone might overhear what he had to say, adjusted his glasses with a nervous gesture, then said in a conspiratorial whisper, "I even had thoughts that Obie might have done in old man Flowers. Dalton Flowers upped and died real sudden like about a month back, but I don't reckon Obie has it in him."

"Heard tell he's mighty good with a shotgun."

"He gets a bug up his ass now and then, thinking everyone's out to jump his claim, but he ain't never found anything worth a bucket of warm spit. Neither of them."

"What do you mean?"

"Obie's as crazy as a bedbug, and Flowers was hardly better. I swear the only talent either of them had was finding worthless holes in the ground."

"So how did Flowers leave his daughters such valuable mining properties?" Slocum asked. The clerk's response—again—was a torrent of laughter.

"He didn't leave those girls of his two dimes to rub together. As to his boy, well, I don't reckon they'd spoken for years. A real ne'er-do-well."

Slocum thought hard about everything he had gleaned. Belle and Corey hadn't inherited anything worth mentioning, or so said the land clerk. But the man had admitted he didn't know what was on the property he recorded. He was a clerk and had no reason to know of the assay from a claim. Slocum worried this over. The clerk had no call to know how rich a claim was, but word got around fast, especially if it was a rich enough strike.

"Could you check this deed to see if it was registered to Clark?"

"Who else would own this? Unless it was Dalton Flowers." The man chuckled at his little joke. Slocum had to be sure the Spit Bucket Mine really belonged to Belle and Corey.

The clerk took down the book with the doctored entry. He opened it and ran his finger down the claims numbers, then shook his head. He turned the book open to the spine, studied it, then matched the number against the deed Slocum had handed him.

"Anything wrong?" Slocum asked, knowing there was.

"I don't understand this. This here deed is the one I gave to Obie for the property, but the ledger entry says it belonged to Dalton Flowers. That don't make a lick of sense. The bad blood between the two rules out any swap of property." The clerk scratched his head.

"It probably doesn't mean anything," Slocum said. He took back the deed and put it into his pocket.

He didn't know what was going on, but he knew one thing for sure. He had killed the real owner of the Spit Bucket Mine so Belle and Corey could sell it for hundreds of thousands of dollars.

7

Slocum stepped into the crowded street and pulled down the brim of his hat to keep the bright sunlight out of his eyes. Familiar voices carried on the gusting wind and drew his attention. The clatter of a buggy drowned out their conversation when they drove past, but Belle and Corey Flowers didn't see him in front of the land office.

He waited for them to go by, then hurried to the stables two streets over. He had to get his own trail clothes stashed with his gear at the stable. The tight clothes Belle had taken out of her upstairs wardrobe were cutting into him uncomfortably in all the wrong places. Slocum wasn't sure what he intended, but by the time he changed his clothes and saddled his gelding, he knew he had to find out more of the Flowers sisters' scheme.

Slocum rode back into the street, stood in the stirrups, and peered around to see if Belle and Corey had stopped somewhere. He didn't see them, and he hadn't expected to. From the intensity of their argument, he guessed they had kept riding. No one got that riled, only to stop and get out of their buggy a few yards down the street. All he had caught were a few words: silver, next mine, shotgun.

Separately, they meant nothing. Taken together, they gave Slocum a suspicion what was going on, and he didn't much like it. Belle was not a stupid woman and had to know she was playing with fire duping men with wealth and power like George Hearst. Slocum had nothing against a little larceny, but anyone stealing from the rich had to know when to take his—or her—chips off the table and run for the hills.

He rode slowly, not wanting to overtake the women. Belle had thought nothing of paying him a thousand dollars for his few minutes of work because she and Corey had raked in three hundred times that much. The way Slocum saw the scam, he was taking as big a risk as they were and ought to get a bigger cut of the money. Belle was a lovely woman and he enjoyed the time he spent with her, but she wasn't worth a third of the take from George Hearst.

The sun baked his face but Slocum didn't pull his brim down to protect his face. He had to keep a sharp eye out for the ruts in the road. The buggy was only one of many heavier wagons traveling this road. He had to study the sides to see if any new tracks led down a side road. If they stayed on the main track down the middle of the canyon, he'd see them soon enough.

It was a little after noon when Slocum saw the narrow-wheeled track cutting away from the main road and heading up into the hills. A large wooden sign told him the road led to the Cuckoo Clock Mine. A few words scrawled in some foreign language—he thought it might be German—completed the sign. Slocum bent over in the saddle and touched his finger to the sign. It came away with smeary white paint. The Cuckoo Clock was a new mine, and he thought he knew who had tended the sign so recently that the paint hadn't had time to dry.

Cutting across country and avoiding the two ruts that passed for a road to the mine, Slocum rode another two miles before he heard Belle and Corey still arguing. He dismounted and left his horse tethered to a juniper where it could crop at sere grass.

Slocum checked his six-shooter and made sure it rested easy in its holster when a third voice chimed in to the argument. A man was telling Belle and Corey they didn't know what they were doing. Keeping low, Slocum advanced until he could stretch belly down on a boulder and get a good look at the mine and the three in front of it.

"You're doing it all wrong. I don't know why the hell it worked. You can't high grade like that. Tease 'em. Sink the hook just a little and then let them bite down on it the rest of the way on their own." The stocky man stood with a shotgun cradled in the crook of his left arm. His right index finger curled around the triggers of the double-barreled weapon.

"It worked, didn't it?" demanded Belle. She stamped her foot as Slocum had seen her do when she was angry. "We might have pressed our luck a little, but we got three hundred fifty thousand."

It surprised Slocum that Belle told this man how much they'd made off George Hearst. If the short, sandy-haired man had been part of the Flowers sisters' plan, why bother hiring an outsider like him? Slocum was glad to get the thousand dollars, but from all he had seen of Belle and Corey, they weren't the kind who spent money needlessly.

This started him thinking in other directions. They'd spend a thousand dollars willingly if it diverted attention from them. The money resting in Slocum's pocket must have been paid to set him up to take the fall if anything went wrong. Slocum didn't see how he could have been blamed, but Belle and Corey were resourceful women. They had something in mind.

The smartest thing he could do was take what he had left and race the wind out of Nevada. Nowhere in the West might be big enough to hide him if Hearst took it into his head that Slocum had rooked him out of the money. Slocum didn't know the details, but he had heard Hearst was partner in a mining company so big it owned most of the profitable mines in the Comstock Lode. The Consolidated Virginia Company said frog and everyone in the district jumped.

"We've covered our tracks," Corey insisted. "And don't blame Belle over the Spit Bucket Mine. That nugget was my idea."

"Don't go worryin' your pretty head over it," the man said. He went to Corey and kissed her on the cheek. Then he kissed Belle and turned toward the narrow mouth of the Cuckoo Clock Mine. "Better get to work. Damn, but I hate this part."

Slocum thought the man must be having an attack of conscience until Belle called, "Wait up. Take this." She fished out a handkerchief and handed it to him.

"Thanks," the man said. "That damned dust makes me choke something fierce."

"It'll be cleared out before his agents arrive, won't it?" asked Corey.

"Don't worry over it. There's quite a draft blowing out from somewhere deep in the mine. I think some fool's dynamited a hole clean through to the top of the hill. It's a wonder the roof didn't cave in when the charge went off."

"Be careful," called Corey as the man vanished into the mine with the shotgun. She turned to her sister and began talking in tones too low for Slocum to overhear.

He flinched and reached for his Colt Navy when the shotgun roared. Slocum settled back onto his belly and watched as dust billowed from the mouth of the mine. He was ready when a second and a third blast echoed from the Cuckoo Clock Mine. The man was salting the mine, loading the shotgun barrel with high grade ore and then blasting it into the rocky mine walls. Anyone making a casual inspection would get excited over the abundance of silver.

Everything fell into place for Slocum. Corey had done the salting at the Spit Bucket Mine and had used too much silver. She had made the mine appear far more valuable than it was—suspiciously valuable, if Hearst's agents had had their wits about them. They were blinded by greed and the women's beauty.

Slocum began to appreciate how the scheme was coming together, but he had to agree with the man doing the salting on the Cuckoo Clock. They had made a good score—a fabulous one—and were pushing their luck to the limit trying to peddle still another worthless mine.

Hearst and his partners in Consolidated Virginia hadn't gotten rich by being forgiving. Hearst wouldn't see this as a valuable lesson learned. He'd want them caught and hanged for the thieves they were.

Slocum ducked back down when the man came from the mine. He had tied Belle's handkerchief around his face like a road agent's mask. Once in the clean mountain air, he took it off and snapped it like a small white whip. Clouds of brown dust popped from it and billowed on the strong breeze blowing from behind him. He handed the now dirty cloth back to Belle.

"That about does it. The rest is in place." The man looked toward a line shack a hundred yards away. "Let's get back to town. The sooner we finish this, the more I'll like it."

Belle and Corey took the shotgun and wrapped it in a blanket before putting it in the rear of their buggy. The man mounted a horse and waited for them. He rode alongside the buggy as they retraced their path on the way back to Virginia City.

Slocum waited for them to round a bend in the road before scrambling down from his vantage point and going to the mine. The dust still hung like a heavy brown fog inside. He used his own bandanna to keep from choking as he made his way inside. It didn't take a mining engineer to see where the silver had been blasted into the walls. Slocum hurried from the mine before his eyes watered any more from the dust.

But the man had been right. This salting was done well. In a day or two, there would be scant evidence left behind that the mine had been salted. Slocum looked at the shack and wondered what the man and the Flowers sisters had been talking about when they said "the rest was in place."

He went to the shack that had been built on the verge of a twenty-foot cliff. At the base were fresh dumpings. Slocum made his way down a narrow path and saw that the pile was taller than his head. Deep ruts showed where a heavily laden wagon had come up the ravine and stopped nearby.

Slocum tried to figure out what was going on. The wagon had brought the tailings. That was the only explanation, but why dump here when it was easier to leave the debris from a mine at the base? He poked through the pile and a slow smile came to his lips. The dross contained higher grade ore than was taken from most mines. This was another, subtler way of salting the mine.

Whoever checked the mine would note the silver on the surface of the walls. They might even use a pick hammer to take a few samples, which could be switched by Belle or Corey on the way back to town. But if they rooted through the tailings, they'd see that the dregs contained high-grade silver.

"A real clever plan, Belle," Slocum said aloud. "Salt the rock *and* the tailings." He'd never heard of anyone doing that. And it seemed to be proof positive that the Cuckoo Clock Mine was worth any price Belle asked. All she had done was shoot a few dollars of silver into the rock and buy high-grade ore from some other mine. It might have even been shipment diverted from its trip down the Washoe Valley to a mill.

Slocum hiked back up the slope and found his horse. He had a bit more to do before he worked his own bit of skulduggery. A thousand dollars was nice. An equal share would be even better.

• • •

He rode faster getting back to Virginia City. Belle and
Corey had a head start, but he knew where they were going.
They'd return to their house up on Gold Hill. The man who
had helped them doctor the mine was more important to
Slocum. He wanted to find out everything he could about
a possible rival for a share in the sale of the Cuckoo
Clock Mine.

The man rode beside the buggy until he was almost back
to town, then picked up the pace and rode ahead. Slocum
had to leave the road or the Flowers sisters would see him.
He circled and came into Virginia City from the west. Luck
rode with him. He saw the man dismounting in front of the
Old Washoe Club, a saloon that had seen better days.

Slocum had to shake off his distaste for the dive. He had
been rich only a day and already he preferred the Union
Club on Nob Hill in San Francisco to this seedy place. He
hitched his horse to a post and climbed onto the rickety
boardwalk in front of the saloon. The Old Washoe Club
was better appointed inside than he would have thought
from the exterior. Ankle-deep sawdust might hide the worst
of the filth, but it smelled sharp and clean and had been
replaced recently.

Behind the bar hung a large picture of a nude reclining woman, almost a duplicate of the one in the Howling
Wilderness. The artist was either prolific or just good at
copying his own work. The bar stretched a good ten yards
down the back of the saloon. A half-dozen men were bellied
up and drinking, mostly beer from the look of it.

"Welcome, stranger. Ain't seen you in here before. Buy
me a drink?" A skinny whore took Slocum's arm and tried
to pull him toward a table near a side door. If he accepted
her invitation, he knew he'd be drinking a Mickey Finn and
would be whisked out the side door where he'd be robbed.
The Old Washoe Club was that kind of place.

"Prefer to drink alone. Sorry," he said insincerely. "I'm
a bit down on my luck and don't have much."

"Not even two bits?" she asked, smiling to show broken, black teeth. "That's all I charge. Ten minutes for two bits." She ran her hand up and down Slocum's arm and smiled even more broadly. "For the likes of you, I'd make it fifteen minutes."

Slocum shook his head. She started to make a lewd comment about his manhood when a new customer pushed through the door and bellowed, "Drinks are on me! I done hit the big one!"

Grateful for the diversion, Slocum accepted his free drink and began moving slowly around the huge room, looking for the man who had been with Belle and Corey at the mine. A doorway opened onto a smaller back room where a half-dozen card tables were set up. The man was sitting with his back to the door, intent on a game of seven-card stud.

Slocum stood and watched a few minutes, trying to get a feel for the man's personality from the way he played. The best Slocum could tell, the man had no idea about odds or common sense, counting on betting wildly on a pair of deuces when either of the others in the game had him beaten ten ways to Sunday.

"Mind if I sit in?" Slocum asked, pulling up a chair. The two playing the man seemed grateful for the chance to get out. They were taking money by the handfuls and it wouldn't be long before the man was drunk enough to accuse them of cheating, although they were simply playing their hands.

"Go on. Be my guest. Let me buy you a drink. Hell, let me buy you a whole damned bottle. I'm feelin' lucky tonight!"

Slocum pulled out a few rumpled greenbacks and put them on the table, all too aware of the thick wad remaining in his pocket. He told himself not to bet more than was already on the table. Accepting the man's drink, he acknowledged it by pushing out a single bill. "That'll get things started," Slocum said.

He didn't have to worry about losing more than the paltry few dollars he had started with. The man lost almost fifty dollars before coming up with an empty poke.

This suited Slocum just fine. "Let me buy you a drink," he said to the man. "It's only right since I seem to have won most of your money." The other players who had drifted in and out of the game seldom remained longer than a hand before leaving. They seemed to know Slocum's opponent and steered clear of him.

"That's a neighborly thing to do. The rest of these sons a' bitches don't have a decent bone in their bodies."

"What's your pleasure . . ." Slocum let the sentence hang, hoping the man would fill in a name. He did and Slocum wasn't too surprised.

"Name's Flowers, Reed Flowers. And I'll have whatever Gus has hidden away behind the bar for his best customers."

Slocum and Reed Flowers went back into the big room of the Old Washoe Club, which was now filled with drunk miners and miners intending to get drunk. They found a table to one side of the room. Slocum fetched a half bottle of rotgut and sat next to Flowers.

"Drink up," Slocum urged. It didn't take much goading for Flowers to begin drinking steadily. He didn't do it any better than he gambled. Before the bottle was gone, he was falling out of his chair. Slocum had to grab him a couple times to keep him from diving facefirst into the sawdust. Slocum hated cheap drunks, and Reed Flowers wasn't doing anything to alter this prejudice.

"They're all ag'in me, they are," moaned Flowers after Slocum propped him up in the chair. "They stole everything."

"Who might this be? Can't the sheriff help you?" Slocum sat back and let the man pour his own whiskey now. He had lost his taste for liquor.

"They bought the damned sheriff. They own the whole damn town, they do." Flowers bent forward as if sharing a deep secret. "It's the thieves that control the whole Comstock mining district. Consolidated Virginia Company."

"Why don't you just ride on out? A man like you has obvious talent. You could—"

"You don't unnerstan'," Flowers protested drunkenly. "They didn't rob me. They robbed my pa. Hearst and the rest of them, they stole everything he had. They ruined him. He died of a broken heart. 'Nuff to break my heart." He sloshed more whiskey into his glass and drained it quickly.

"Mines? They stole mining property from him?" Slocum knew the answer he'd get.

"Every last one. Not enough that there are claim jumpers who take the valuable mines. These men—Hearst and Sutro and the rest of those bastards—wait like vultures. Work like a son of a bitch all your life, break your back to get a good claim and make a decent living, and down they swoop!"

Reed Flowers's eyes glazed over, and he sank to the table. Slocum sat and stared at him. He felt nothing for the man. Even if Dalton Flowers had been robbed blind, he would have disinherited Reed. No father appreciates a son like this who could go through a fortune inside a few weeks.

Slocum left Reed Flowers snoring raggedly and went into the cold night air of Virginia City. He had a powerful lot of thinking to do.

8

"I'd say he's one lying son of a sidewinder," the land office clerk said. He scratched his chin, pushed his bifocal glasses back up onto his thin nose, and then snorted in contempt. "But then, I reckon you've been talking to Reed Flowers. Calling him a rattler is doing a disservice to every snake I ever met."

Slocum's head threatened to split apart like a frozen melon. He hadn't drunk that much of the vile whiskey at the Old Washoe Club, but he still had the grandfather of all hangovers. He found it hard to listen to the clerk and concentrate on figuring out what it all meant.

"So Dalton Flowers never had anything for Hearst and the other partners in Consolidated Virginia to steal?"

"Not saying that. Not at all, since I've heard of stranger things than Flowers hitting upon a decent claim. He was all the time out there digging and bragging. Mostly, he was bragging, just like that good-for-nothing son of his." The clerk coughed politely and looked at Slocum carefully. "You been asking some strange questions. What's your angle, mister?"

Slocum forced himself to look the clerk squarely in the

eye and not glance toward the ledger sitting on the desk. He wondered if the land clerk had been examining the forgery Belle and Corey had done, or if it being on the desk was just circumstance. Since Slocum didn't believe in coincidence, he had to believe the clerk was trying to figure out what was going on. Asking all these questions was only goading him to continue his investigation.

And when he came to the conclusion Slocum already had reached, the clerk would go trotting over to the sheriff's office and ask that justice be done.

Justice might be served even sooner if Hearst caught wind of Belle and Corey's scheme to defraud him. Reed Flowers was the obvious weak link, what with his heavy drinking and terrible gambling. Slocum hadn't asked around but he figured Dalton Flowers's only son was big with the ladies, too, whoring around Virginia City and bragging.

"Let's just say I'm interested in seeing Obadiah Clark's claim properly noted."

"And why would that be? Haven't seen Obie in a coon's age. You know him?" The clerk fixed Slocum with a hard stare, as if daring him to admit he had killed the crazy old prospector and buried him at the Spit Bucket Mine.

Slocum wasn't about to confess to the killing, even if it had been in self-defense. Slocum paused for a moment as that raced through his mind. The lunatic old geezer had opened fire on him, and he would have left Clark alone except for the shotgun blasts. Slocum had only returned fire, but he wouldn't have even been at the mine if Belle hadn't sent him there. She had to know Clark was going to open fire on anyone. The man was obsessed with claim jumpers—and it turned out he had every right to be wary.

"Haven't seen him around, either. Just think of me as a friend."

The clerk snorted in disgust and turned back to his ledger. Slocum saw that the clerk went past the forgery and noted different numbers and names at the bottom of the page. Slocum let out a little sigh of relief. Business was going on, and nobody much cared about the bit of forgery that had been done on the deed for a worthless mine. Nobody except George Hearst.

Slocum considered letting the mining magnate know of Belle's part, then pushed it from his mind. He owed Belle and Corey nothing. The two lovely women had been using him, but he had been paid well for his time. Slocum touched the wad of bills tucked into his shirt pocket. There might be more, lots more, if he played this hand properly.

Hiking up C Street to Union, he heard the Melodian still going strong although it was close to ten in the morning. The show they put on wasn't going to stop until the last miner had spent his last nickel. Slocum turned uphill toward Gold Hill and the fancy houses. As he walked he worried over all he had found out.

Not much made sense. If Dalton Flowers hadn't been as filthy rich as Belle claimed, how could she and Corey afford such a fine house? Had they swindled someone else before Hearst to get the money? Slocum shuddered at the notion of everyone in Virginia City coming after them. The mere thought of hemp rope caused his neck to itch.

Swindling one man who wasn't likely to miss the money didn't strike Slocum as being much of a crime. He had done worse in his day. But it was rank foolishness to think you could get away with the same scheme more than once, no matter what the stakes.

He stopped and looked up the terraced steps to the house. In broad daylight it appeared even more opulent than it had the first time he'd been here. Slocum pushed through the iron gate, went up the steps, and knocked on the gilt-edged door. He heard soft voices inside, then the shuffle of bare feet on polished wood floor. The lace curtain on the door's single window pulled back and a blue eye peered out at him before vanishing.

The door opened and Corey greeted him by throwing her arms around his neck and giving him a big kiss.

"John, you finally came by! We thought something horrible had happened. This is such a lawless town."

He gently disengaged her, thoughts other than the mine swindle flashing through his mind. Slocum had to tell himself to keep to the straight and narrow and not complicate things. Belle was more than a handful. Corey would be more than a bedful, he guessed.

"Came by to talk to Belle. Is she here?"

Corey pouted and looked at him from under lowered lids. "And I thought you'd come by to see me. Oh, well," she said, her mercurial mood shifting. "Belle's upstairs. She'll be done in a few minutes. Help yourself to some breakfast."

Corey showed him into the dining room where a plate of eggs and bacon had been put down. Slocum saw from the other plate at the table that Corey was about finished.

"Don't want to take Belle's breakfast."

"I'll fix her more. She's always saying she eats too much. Can't tell it from looking at her. Don't you think she's a mite on the skinny side? Not like me." Corey pirouetted about, her hands moving slowly over her flaring hips. She laughed like a schoolgirl and quickly sat down, having gotten the desired reaction from him.

Slocum sank down into the chair, realizing how hungry he was. He hadn't eaten breakfast that morning, his belly rumbling like a freight train. The haze of bad liquor was wearing off and left him famished. Slocum gobbled down the eggs and silently took a biscuit when Corey passed them to him. She watched him eat until he asked, "Never seen anyone who was hungry?"

"I love it when a man has appetites and knows how to sate them," she said. She moved slightly, and Slocum felt her leg brushing his under the table.

"Didn't you say Belle was going to be down soon?" Slocum finished the last of the breakfast and leaned back.

"She might have gone out. Really, John, there's nothing you'd want to say to her that you can't say to me."

"You two work as partners, don't you?" He remembered how they had teamed up against Hearst's agents. Neither of the men had a chance once the Flowers sisters started in on them.

"Belle and I have always had an understanding," Corey said, boldly staring at him. "We share and share alike."

Slocum felt like a prize heifer being auctioned off to the highest bidder, and at the same time his pulse accelerated. Corey Flowers was one lovely woman—and he had wondered more than once how different she might prove to be from her darker-haired sister.

"You look upset over something, John," the blonde went on. "How can I make it all better?"

"Obadiah Clark," he said, watching her closely. Her blue eyes widened in surprise. The emotion passed quickly. With very little practice, Corey would make a fine poker player, he decided. She hid her shock well at hearing the man's name.

"Belle told me about your run-in with him. Imagine him using a shotgun like that. But then he always was as crazy as a bedbug."

"You and Belle set me up—you set up Clark," Slocum accused.

"Whatever do you mean? We had no idea he'd be at the mine. And we certainly didn't think he'd try to gun you down. No one's that cracked."

"I'm not a hired gun, and I don't kill for money."

"John," she said earnestly, moving around the table and kneeling by his side, "I know that. Belle and I know it. But you're not a man who gets pushed around easily, either. *That's* what we need. We're dealing with dangerous men, and I don't mean gunslingers."

"I'm going." He stood and started to leave. He'd had enough. Slocum stopped when he heard Corey sobbing softly. He turned and saw her still on her knees, tears running down her cheeks.

"We need you, John. We do!"

"I know you forged the deed to the Spit Bucket Mine to make it seem as if you had title." Slocum pulled out the deed he'd taken from Clark. "Obadiah Clark was the real owner. You used me to jump another man's claim. You used me to kill him."

"No!" Corey wailed. "It's not like that at all." The ring of sincerity in her voice made Slocum hesitate.

"So how is it?" he asked, knowing he shouldn't be asking. He should be leaving Virginia City.

Still on her knees, tears pouring from her blue eyes, Corey sobbed out, "Clark's the claim jumper," she said. "That was Papa's mine, and Clark stole it from him. But we didn't know he would be at the mine. Belle didn't, I didn't. We didn't want you killing anyone."

"So you're saying you just stole it back?" Slocum saw nothing wrong if it were true. He had no way of telling.

"We need money badly, John. We are poverty-stricken. Taking money from the like of George Hearst ought not be a crime. He's got more money than Croesus and won't miss the paltry amount we took."

"Three hundred fifty thousand isn't paltry," Slocum said.

"Maybe not for you, but Belle and I are used to the finer things in life. Papa was rich once, but he died poor as a church mouse. I won't live hand-to-mouth. I won't!"

Again he heard the ring of truth in Corey's words. He started to tell her that he had seen her brother salting the Cuckoo Clock Mine when the blonde slowly stood and took two deliberate steps toward him.

"You're not lily-pure, John Slocum," she accused, eyes flashing like lightning. "You've stolen money in your day. I can see it in your face. Is what we did so wrong?"

He started to answer but the words were cut off. Corey threw her arms around his neck and kissed him hard. Slocum knew better than to get involved with her like this.

In spite of common sense telling him different, he returned the kiss with as much passion as it was given. And he liked it.

"You're just like us, John, and we can be rich together. I'll cut you in on everything. You're taking the risks just as we are. You deserve it."

"A third?" he asked, surprised to hear himself speaking. Greed and lust were dueling for supremacy and both had pushed aside good sense. If Corey was promising him a third of what they'd already swindled, that was more than a hundred thousand dollars. Slocum started to ask about Reed Flowers when Corey kissed him again.

The battle between greed and lust flowed the other way. Corey kissed him fervently and then nibbled at his ear, whispering hotly, "You can be a full partner—in everything we do."

She moved against him like a cat, then wrapped her leg around his waist. Standing on tiptoe, Corey rubbed herself up and down on his thigh. Every movement made him a tad more uncomfortable until he felt strangled in his pants.

He wasn't sure exactly how she did it but Corey managed to unbutton his shirt and get him out of his gun belt before he knew it. Then she dropped to her knees again and looked up longingly at him.

"I want you, John. Do you want me as much?" She reached out and tugged down his drawers. He snapped out stiffly, silently answering her. Corey moved forward and her ruby lips brushed the tip of his manhood. But this wasn't what she wanted.

Arms wrapped around his body, she pressed forward. Slocum lost his balance and tried to step back. Her arms prevented it. He went down hard, the woman swarming over him, kissing and licking as she went. When Corey got back to his mouth, she kissed him harder than before. Her tongue snaked from her mouth into his and erotically dueled before coyly retreating.

Slocum panted harshly now, fully aroused. He gasped when she reached down and caught him. Her slender fingers squeezed hard and began stroking.

"Don't," he said. "That's not what I want."

She grinned wickedly and licked her lips. "That's not what I want, either." She released her grip and stood amid a swirl of her skirts. Corey shrugged her shoulders and got out of her blouse. Slocum was so captivated by the sight of her small, firm breasts that he never quite knew how she got out of her skirt.

She stepped forward and straddled him, the dewy blond triangle between her thighs beckoning to him.

"See what you do want?" she teased. Corey moaned softly when he reached out and ran his fingers up the insides of her legs, stroking and kneading as he went. She quivered and sank down slowly.

Slocum positioned himself to hit her dead center when she collapsed all the way to his crotch. They both groaned with desire as he vanished all the way into her humid interior. Corey bent forward and allowed him to cup her apple-sized breasts in both hands, then rocked back and brought her feet up to either side of his hips.

She leaned back and moved around him in ways that stretched and pulled, stroked and tormented. He felt the pressures building inside his body and she moved up and down on his length, slowly at first, then with more speed. Somehow, she gripped down around him as if she had him in a velvet glove.

"You are so big, John. You fill me up so much, so damned much!" Corey's hips exploded in a frenzy of motion. She worked up and down until friction burned at their privates and ignited a fuse Slocum couldn't stop. He erupted into her clinging interior just as she shrieked out her own joy.

"Oh, John, John," she sobbed. "So good. I've never felt it this much before." She kept moving until he turned limp. Corey sank down, sweat pouring off her face and body. She smiled almost shyly, then bent forward again and rested her head in the hollow of his neck.

Her soft, warm breath gusted across his skin and tickled his ear.

"We'll make a great team, John. We will. Equal partners,

though I don't see how you could have ever enjoyed this near as much as I did." Corey sighed again and snuggled even closer.

Slocum knew the web being spun around him, and it didn't much matter at the moment. Money. Sex. Those were the things that drove men. He tried to tell himself he saw the dangers and accepted them.

He knew he was lying to himself. And it didn't matter.

9

Slocum left Corey, wondering where Belle was. She hadn't been upstairs getting ready for breakfast or she would have come down when Slocum and Corey started their lovemaking. Slocum paused and looked back at the house, and knew he was sinking into quicksand. Being played for a sucker wasn't something that set well with him, and no amount of sex could hold him.

It might work with the agents working for Hearst, but it didn't with him. Slocum circled the house and saw a horse tethered there. He went up the back steps, moving slowly to keep the wood from creaking under his weight. Slocum peered in the kitchen window.

Reed Flowers was collapsed over the large table there. Corey came in, adjusting her clothing. She looked down at her brother and heaved a sigh. The rise and fall of her breasts brought back sudden memories that Slocum pushed away. Corey—and Belle—used their sex like a man used a six-shooter.

"Wake up," Corey said, shaking her brother. He grumbled and shook his head. He had obviously been on one hell of a binge to be this hung over. He tried to push his sister away. She grabbed his wrist and swung him around.

"Drink the coffee, dammit," she said. She poured steaming coffee into a cup and shoved it at Reed. Corey sat and stared at him. Slocum tried to figure out what she was feeling toward her brother. He couldn't do it.

"You shoulda been there, Corey darlin'," Reed said. "We had one hoot, I tell ya."

"What have you been telling people?" she demanded. "You know Belle and I don't like it when you get drunk and start bragging about how rich you're going to be."

"Hell, I *am* rich. Or will be, whenever that skinflint Hearst pays you for the first two mines." He sipped at the coffee and made a face, then took a bigger drink.

Slocum saw a hint of contempt for the first time on Corey's face. And he didn't have to be a genius to know the sisters hadn't told Reed they'd already collected the money from Hearst. If he had been given his cut, he'd be painting the town until he drowned in liquor or lost every penny in wild poker games. Such behavior would alert Hearst—and then the cat would be out of the bag.

And Belle and Corey would have to move on quickly or be put in jail for being the swindlers they were.

"You need a wet nurse, that's what you need," Corey said. "Try not to get into too much trouble. Belle's due back anytime now. The big deal's about set up, and we don't want you rocking the boat until we're ready."

Slocum blinked at this. The *big* swindle was just getting set up? And did he want to be a part of it? He didn't kid himself. If there was any problem, he'd be the one landing in jail. Belle and Corey would protect their drunken brother, however much it cost. Blood was thicker than water.

But a *big* payoff? Slocum couldn't begin to imagine how much was involved. The Comstock was an incredible source of wealth. Slocum had heard men talk of $500,000,000 in silver and gold taken out of the ground. What was a few hundred thousand dollars compared to such a staggering total?

He walked away as softly as he had approached the kitchen window. Reed Flowers's horse neighed but calmed quickly when Slocum kept walking. Slocum didn't slow down until he reached the street in front of the house. A buggy was driving up. He couldn't turn and find a place to hide quick enough. Belle spotted him.

"John! Wait," she called. She tapped the reins against the horse's rump just enough to walk it forward and come even with Slocum. "Were you at the house?"

Slocum didn't know exactly how to answer that. He didn't want to admit doing with Corey what he had already done with Belle, but he didn't know what secrets the women had between themselves. Maybe none, maybe a lot. Corey had always given him the impression she wanted him to herself, but Slocum wasn't going to risk guessing wrong.

"Yep," he said, not wanting to get too deep into it. "You weren't there."

"Things are going well, John." Belle was flushed and excited, but he didn't think she was going to tell him why. "I wish there was time to tell you everything, but . . ."

"I'll be back later. I've got a few matters to tend to. Meet you for dinner?" Slocum suggested, almost hoping Belle would say no.

"Excellent, John. Perfect. I'll meet you at our café." Her brown eyes sparkled. Slocum didn't have to ask which she considered "our café" since it must be where he'd first met Belle and Corey.

Slocum tipped his hat as Belle urged her horse toward the house on the hill. Slocum watched and wondered what was going on. He decided it was time to be sure he had every possibility covered—and that meant double-crossing Belle and Corey, if the need arose.

He walked back to the stable where he saddled his horse and changed into the tight-fitting clothes Belle had given him, considering all the trails he could ride. The lure of money—*big* money, Corey had said—lured him. He knew greed got more men hung than anything else, except possibly getting involved with a woman. And he was up to his ears in that bog, too. Twice over, with Belle and Corey. Mixed into the stew was Reed Flowers. Whatever Belle and Corey were planning, their brother might jinx the entire swindle.

There was a narrow line to walk, and Slocum intended to try. He wanted in on the swindle, even more than the thousand dollars he had received by going to the mines with Hearst's agents. This was the chance of a lifetime. But he wasn't going to spend the rest of his life in jail because of the plot, either.

Slocum went to George Hearst's office and took a deep breath. Settled, he went into the office. The secretary looked up. From the way Watkins frowned, Slocum knew he was trying to place him. The first time Slocum had been here, he'd been dressed for the trail. The secretary had never seen him in his "engineer's" clothes.

"What is it?" Watkins asked brusquely.

"I need to see Mr. Hearst about the properties he's planning to purchase."

"You selling? He's not interested."

"These are mines being purchased from the Flowers sisters. I need to talk to him about the assay from the mines."

"He's busy."

"He strikes me as a man who's always interested in making money—or not losing what he has," Slocum said. "If you don't think he's interested, so be it."

"You know something about the new mines?" The man's attitude was changing just a little. That was enough for Slocum to do some bluffing.

"Never mind. It wouldn't do to disturb him."

"A moment, sir." The secretary went into Hearst's office. The thick fog of cigar smoke coming from inside showed Hearst was puffing away heavily. Slocum heard a grumble and then the secretary bustled out and motioned for Slocum.

"What is it, man?" demanded Hearst. He sat behind a desk cluttered with papers. Slocum saw several deeds pulled open and cigar ashes dropped on the paper. Hearst frowned a moment, trying to place Slocum. It was obvious he couldn't.

"I just wanted to inquire about some problems with the assay off the Silver Canary and the Spit Bucket. Your men might have gotten the numbers wrong."

"Why's that? I only hire the best." Hearst rocked back in his chair and knocked more ash from his thick cigar. "There's nothing amiss with the ore out of those mines. I'm sure of it."

"I could be wrong," Slocum said, hoping he had covered himself enough if—when—Hearst found that he had bought worthless holes in the ground. "Have been before, will be again, but if you'd just check I'd feel a mite easier."

Hearst grumbled and pawed through the papers on his desk until he came up with a scrap of paper. His finger stabbed down like an Apache arrow sinking into a blue-coat's back.

"Here," Hearst said. "Not quite four thousand dollars a ton out of the Spit Bucket Mine and just at three thousand dollars a ton from the Silver Canary. Not the bonanza that came out of the Ophir way back when, but then what is?"

"Those are your numbers or ones given by the Flowers sisters?"

"What do those two little ladies know of assay? Hell, man, of course they are my numbers. My agents aren't fools. I don't tolerate fools."

"Sorry to have bothered you." Slocum left quickly, Hearst growling like a grizzly coming out from a long winter's hibernation. He hurried outside and felt the hot wind gusting through Virginia City erase the sweat beading his forehead. How had Belle falsified the assay results? Neither mine was half as rich as Hearst indicated.

Slocum snorted in disgust. Neither mine had four thousand dollars' worth of silver left in it, much less in any given ton of ore. Whatever had been done, Hearst was still satisfied and on the hook to be bilked some more.

He had done all he could to warn the man, and Hearst refused to examine the properties himself. As Slocum walked toward the Howling Wilderness for a much needed drink, he wondered if Belle and Corey had gotten a look at the assay reports coming back and had somehow forged them, too. He had seen both women with Hearst's agents. They might have sweet-talked the men into showing them the results.

Slocum shook his head. This was a dangerous game if the agents had been bought off, either with money or sex. Too many people knowing about the swindle spelled sure disaster.

Entering the Howling Wilderness Saloon, Slocum recoiled from the heat inside. The place was packed to the walls, everyone drinking anything put in front.

"What's the occasion?" Slocum asked, forcing his way through to the bar. The barkeep shook his head and pointed to his ears. He couldn't hear over the din. Slocum shouted his question again.

"Free drinks for everybody. Here, mister." The barkeep poured a big drink and hurried on to keep the rest of the patrons' glasses brimming. Slocum sampled the whiskey and found it much better than the rotgut served at the Old Washoe Club.

"Who's doing the buying?" he asked the miner pressing hard against him at the bar. "I'd like to thank him."

"No need. This cayuse has more money than sense," the miner said. "Claims he hit it rich."

"Claims? You don't think he did?"

"Reed Flowers hit it rich? Ha!"

Slocum stood on tiptoe and saw Belle and Corey's brother at the other end of the bar, whores hanging on both arms and a stack of bills in front of him. Belle must have given him some of their ill-gotten gains, probably to keep him quiet. That obviously hadn't worked. He was celebrating success and might be putting them all in jail with his wild ways.

10

Slocum left the saloon, not wanting to be in the same place with Reed Flowers. The man didn't even notice he'd been there since the Howling Wilderness was so crowded. The more Slocum saw of Flowers, the less he liked him—and the more he worried he would jinx the swindle Belle and Corey had worked out. Slocum just wished he knew more about the women's intentions.

He wandered the streets of Virginia City, taking in the prosperity and seeing how many of the miners lived. The crashing poverty was in such stark contrast to the opulence of the opera house and other buildings that had been rebuilt after last year's fire that Slocum found himself coming to a conclusion about what to do much more slowly than usual.

Making up his mind had never caused Slocum much problem before. Things tended to be good or bad, and all it took choosing between them was to decide what he wanted most and devil take the hindmost. This time was different. Belle and Corey were playing a dangerous game, but one that might get them all a fabulous amount of money in a hurry.

The wild card was their brother.

Slocum wanted the money and was willing to tolerate the hazards of getting it. He smiled crookedly and shook his head. He didn't want to admit this, but he wanted both the women, too. He'd never found such a lively pair before, nor was he likely to anytime soon.

"If you run with the thoroughbreds, you have to be as fast as they are," Slocum muttered to himself.

The poverty of the miners and the wealth of the men owning the mines were all around him. He knew which side of the fence he wanted to live on. He spent the rest of the day catching up on sleep and was at the café a full ten minutes before Belle showed.

"John, I hope you haven't been waiting long," she said, greeting him. She grabbed his hand and held it in both of hers. Slocum thought she was going to straighten up and kiss him, which would be decidedly improper public behavior, but she didn't. "Let's go in and eat. I am famished."

Slocum got them a table toward the back, but Belle insisted on the one in the window so they could see out— and everyone passing by on the boardwalk could see them. This made Slocum a bit edgy. He preferred to sit with his back to a wall and be sure who could see him.

"I want the table in the back," he said.

"Nonsense, we have nothing to hide. I want everyone in Virginia City to know I'm having dinner with the handsomest man in the district."

"The Irish have a word for that," Slocum said.

"What's that?" Belle asked, her gaze locking with his.

"Blarney."

She laughed as if he had made the funniest joke in the world, but she still guided him to the table in front of the window. She pulled the linen napkin down to her lap and smiled at Slocum.

This time he had real money to pay the bill. But the eleven hundred dollars he had received from Belle was going fast. That was the problem with money, Slocum decided. If you had it, you spent it. If you didn't have it, you never knew what you were missing.

In a way, he might be better off being dirt poor again.

"We'll be rich, John," Belle said softly so that only he could hear. "We will make this work, and we will be richer than our wildest dreams."

"What are we going to do to get it?" Slocum asked. "Sell more mines you've salted?"

"Now, John, Mr. Hearst is an intelligent man. His agents are capable. They know what they're buying."

"Those mines are worthless, leastwise compared to what he paid for them. The Silver Canary isn't a bad claim, but it's been worked so's the best ore has been taken."

"Oh, poo, John. All that's water under the bridge. We have other fish to fry now."

"Have you done this before?" Slocum asked. The waiter took their order. Slocum found himself thinking about the steak he ordered as much as he did Belle's history. He wasn't sure she would ever tell him the truth anyway.

"Live well?" she parried. "Of course, and I intend to continue."

Slocum shook his head. "This is a mighty dangerous game. I think I'm going to be content with my winnings and just cash in."

"No, John, you can't!" she protested. "We need you." In a lower voice, she added, "*I* need you."

"I can't work blind. That's the way to end up with a noose around my neck." He stared outside at the lights along Virginia City's streets. The darkness hid the poverty and accentuated the richness.

"You'll be my right-hand man, John. That's how much I need you." Belle sounded sincere, but Slocum reckoned she'd had a lot of practice. Still, even a small piece of the pie would sate his hunger for some time.

"What do I have to do?"

"First, eat that delicious-looking Delmonico steak, then we'll get you some real clothes. Those just won't do any longer. They fit you so poorly. Then we're going to the opera. I'll tell you all about it as we go."

Slocum kept trying to turn the conversation toward Belle's new scheme, but she was too intent on the opera. He finally gave up and decided to play a waiting game. Even through the fitting of a gray swallowtail coat and britches too tight to be comfortable, Slocum said little. Somehow, Belle seemed to think getting him all decked out in fancy duds of his own was going to be of some benefit.

Slocum wasn't so sure. He had been gussied up like this before and had never enjoyed it.

"So, John, what do you think of your clothing? I believe you are even more handsome than ever, and I hadn't thought that was possible."

"I'm not going to leave my six-shooter behind," he said, settling the cross-draw holster on his hip. It made a bulge under the showy coat and was hard to get out fast, should the need arise.

"Don't," she said, smiling like a kitten with a bowl of cream. Slocum had the feeling that no matter what he did, it was going to please Belle. And it wasn't because she was wild in love with him—it was because he kept playing her game without knowing the rules.

"Let's go," he said, grateful that she had paid for his clothes when he saw the tailor's bill.

"The opera is not something to hurry to so it will be over quicker," she said almost primly. "It is to be savored, enjoyed." They walked down the street. Miners hooted and called to Belle and made disparaging remarks about Slocum. He ignored them, and Belle might have been in a different world for all the heed she paid the crude comments.

But Slocum found the way down Union Street to Piper's Opera House blocked when two miners stepped out, cold fury burning in their eyes.

"We want our money," the taller one said. Slocum was six feet one and felt dwarfed by the towering miner. Hardrock men tended to be short and stout, needing to spend long hours hunched over in cramped tunnels.

"Do get out of our way, sir," Belle said. She made a brushing motion with her hand as if this would remove the man from her sight. Slocum saw immediately this was no bug to get swept away. The giant miner was a problem, and his truculent companion was even worse. The man had lost an eye in some accident and a knife scar ran from ear to ear across his throat. This one had escaped death and didn't show the least bit of fear, even when Slocum gave him a cold look and moved his coattail away from his pistol.

"The money. He owes it."

Since the man was staring at Belle, Slocum knew Reed Flowers had been in another poker game and had welshed on his loss.

Belle looked from the miner to Slocum and back. He saw just a hint of apprehension on her face, and he knew why. She and her sister had gone to great lengths not to mention Reed. Slocum didn't know why, other than the man was a wastrel. Belle must not have known he had been asking around and had crossed her brother's slimy trail in a dozen different ways.

"The lady and I don't owe you anything," Slocum said. The shorter man grinned wickedly and rocked back, his fist cocking behind his head as he judged the distance between his fist and Slocum's jaw.

Slocum surprised him. The man expected such a dandy to back away in horror—and get his jaw broken when a fist like a sledgehammer hit it. Slocum took a quick step forward, his left fist traveling less than two inches. The shock echoed all the way up his arm as he hit what felt like solid rock.

The one-eyed miner gasped and unleashed his own attack, but it sailed by Slocum's head because his target had closed rather than retreated. A second quick jab took the man's breath away. Slocum followed it with a right and then another left. By this time, the miner's gut had taken too much of a pounding. He slumped to his knees, grasping out weakly to support himself against Slocum.

A well-placed kick knocked the man out.

Belle let out a cry of warning as the giant growled like a grizzly and reached out huge arms to catch up Slocum in a bear hug. Slocum ducked under the powerful grab and tried the same tactic. If he'd thought he was pounding rock with the other miner's belly, Slocum knew he was trying to drive his hand through a steel plate now.

"I want my money. He owes two hundred dollars!" bellowed the miner. He lumbered around to make another grab at Slocum.

Slocum knew he might be able to wear the man down through superior speed, but matching strengths would only end up one way. Slocum didn't want a crushed spine so he whipped out his Colt Navy in a smooth motion, cocked it, and pointed it square between the man's eyes.

"You owe me," the giant repeated. Slocum began to wonder if the man was a little daft.

"I'll pay you off with a slug in the head if you don't back away," Slocum promised. His finger was tightening on the hair trigger to stop the miner's advance when he heard the clatter of boots behind him.

"Jed, now don't you go botherin' these people," came a sharp command.

"Don't go gettin' involved where you don't belong, Sheriff," Jed said. He waved arms like huge timbers back and forth and started toward Slocum again.

"Don't do it, mister," the sheriff said. "We'll handle this."

"Do it quick or he's buzzard bait," Slocum said.

Two ropes whirled through the air, one from Slocum's left and the other from the right. The lariats dropped over Jed's shoulders and tightened. The two deputies started a tug of war. Even against two strapping lawmen, the miner gave a good account of himself. Only when the sheriff pushed in front of Slocum and Belle and swung the long-barreled shotgun around did Jed quiet.

"Sorry this happened," the sheriff said. "If y'all are headin' for the opera house, you'd better get on in. I'll see that old Jed here sleeps off his mad." He gestured to the deputies, who pulled their roped prisoner along behind them. Slocum saw how both men kept their distance. He figured they had done this before, probably with Jed.

"I do declare," Belle said, using her fan to vigorously cool herself. "Whatever was all that about?"

Slocum almost told her, then stopped. He needed an ace in the hole. Pretending to be ignorant of Reed Flowers's wild ways was probably more of a deuce or a trey, but it was better than nothing.

"Drunk miners do the damnedest things," he said. "Let's forget about the opera and—" Slocum was cut off in midsentence when Belle called out to a couple entering the theater.

"Oh, hello there, Mr. Hearst. How are you this fine evening? You'll never guess what just happened to us."

Belle pulled Slocum along to greet the mining magnate and a young, well-dressed woman whom Slocum doubted was the walruslike man's wife. Hearst looked irritated that Belle approached him, but he smiled and touched the brim of his silk hat.

"Evening, Miss Flowers." Hearst fixed his cold stare on Slocum. "Sir."

Slocum kept quiet, wondering what to do. He hoped Hearst would say nothing about their earlier meeting and how Slocum had tried to warn him away from buying anything more from Belle.

"We're looking forward to this fine performance, aren't you?" Belle asked, moving to block Hearst's entry into the theater.

"Yes."

The man's terseness told Slocum that Hearst separated pleasure from business and saw Belle as pushing her own financial interests.

"Afterward, shall we get together for a genteel drink?" Belle suggested. Slocum was shocked at her boldness. Hearst didn't seem to notice, and the woman with him was amused.

"I am otherwise engaged with a game of cards," Hearst said.

"Excellent. Mr. Slocum is an expert player." Belle started to say more but Slocum gripped her arm. He wasn't going to get into a high-stakes game with the likes of George Hearst. The mining magnate could spend hundreds of thousands of dollars. What would he consider a penny-ante game of poker? Slocum had heard the tales of thousands of dollars being bet on a single draw of the cards.

Then he smiled as he remembered he had won heavily on his first night in Virginia City with a similar game.

"Perhaps you can join me?" Hearst looked Slocum over, as if he were seeing him for the first time. "You've got spirit. Do you have the skill at cards to go with it?"

"Of course," Belle cut in.

"I've played a hand or two," Slocum said, heading Belle off from getting him in any deeper.

"At the Cassandra Club after the opera," Hearst said, sidestepping Belle and entering the lobby.

"What's this about?" Slocum asked. "I don't have enough money to even sit down with Hearst and his cronies."

"I've always wanted to see the Cassandra Club," Belle said, as if she hadn't heard him. "It is the richest private club in the district. All the powerful men go there."

"I'm not risking my money in a poker game. Hearst probably bets more on a single turn of the cards than I've ever seen in my life."

"Oh, John, don't be such a spoilsport. If you want to fly with the eagles, you've got to spread your wings. I have confidence in you." Belle smiled and took his arm, almost pulling him into the opera.

Slocum sat stoically, trying to figure out why anyone liked fat women caterwauling like heifers stuck in mud. Belle appeared to enjoy the singing; Slocum's mind wandered. He was a good poker player, but he knew the key to winning was to have enough stake to weather temporary setbacks. It was sometimes necessary to lose several small hands to rake in the big pot.

"Let's go, John."

"What? Why?" Slocum looked around and saw the others in the theater leaving. He had completely shut out the opera.

"It's time to make some money. Do you feel lucky tonight?"

Slocum didn't answer directly. Being forced to sit through two hours of funny-dressed people singing in some language he didn't understand—while wearing a celluloid collar—struck him as being as much fun as getting shot in the foot.

"I do. Look. There's Hearst's carriage. If we hurry we might be able to go into the club with him."

"Why is this important?" Slocum asked. Belle wanted to be seen with Hearst and to get inside the Cassandra Club for some reason. It had to have something to do with her new deal. "Are we looking for someone else to buy your salted mine?"

"Now, John, that's no way to talk about valuable mining property. Someone might overhear you and think it's worthless. The Cuckoo Clock Mine is a mighty fine buy for what I'm asking."

They hailed a passing carriage for hire and arrived at the club a few minutes after Hearst. Belle hurried up the broad marble steps to the front door where a liveried servant waited. He looked her over and smiled slightly. When the doorman saw Slocum, his expression hardened.

"May I help you?" the doorman asked in a frosty voice.

"We're with Mr. Hearst," Belle said. "Oh, look, there he is now!" Belle waved to Hearst as he handed his coat to another servant. The mining magnate grinned and motioned Belle inside. The doorman stepped back but watched Slocum like a roadrunner watching a rattler for the right time to strike.

"So pleased you could come," Hearst said. "I'm ready for cards. Are you?" Hearst looked at Slocum as he took out a thick wallet and began fanning through the sheaf of greenbacks stuffed there. Slocum saw only hundred-dollar bills. Hearst was carrying several thousand dollars. Thoughts of drawing his Colt Navy and robbing him flashed through Slocum's mind. It would be easier than playing poker. He could be out of town in ten minutes and miles away from the Comstock district by sunrise.

"Certainly," said Belle, reaching into her purse. Slocum tried not to show surprise when she pulled out a wad of bills rivaling Hearst's.

"Park you gun and let's get down to it," said Hearst. He pointed to a checkroom. Hearst turned and went into the main salon. The servant who had taken Hearst's coat appeared and waited for Slocum to shuck off his gun belt. Slocum reluctantly passed over his Colt, but he knew he'd only draw more attention than he wanted if he refused.

"I'll bankroll you, John. Just don't lose. I need the money for—" Belle stopped and shrugged. "I just need it."

"I don't know what kind of player Hearst is. He might be better than I am. He's got the money to outlast me."

"Win early," Belle urged. She gave the room a quick once over and ignored the opulence. Slocum had seen fancy clubs before. The Union Club was a hovel compared to the Cassandra Club. Gilt everywhere, marble and mirrors and red crushed velvet hangings and pictures on the wall that looked very expensive. Slocum was no judge but the building and its furnishings might have cost upward of a million dollars.

"Sit, sit," urged Hearst, pointing to an empty chair across from him. The other three men in the game chomped on cigars and puffed frequently, sending blue clouds of smoke into the air. "Draw poker, nothing wild. Simple. One-hundred-dollar ante, no table limit. Agreed?"

"Get on with it, George. We know the rules," said a weaselly man to Slocum's left. "Heaven alone knows we've played often enough."

Slocum glanced at Belle, wondering if she understood what this meant. If these men played often, they knew each other's style. Even if they didn't consciously team up against him, Slocum knew he was at an even bigger disadvantage. They could lose a hand or two and figure they'd get it back next week or next month. They didn't have to win tonight.

The deal went quickly. Five-card draw was an easy game for Slocum to assess the odds. What he had to feel out was the style of play of the others at the table. Two he dismissed after four hands. They were interested only in social playing, lacking the killer instinct. The weaselly man and Hearst, however, were different.

For them winning was everything. They had all the money any man could ever want, so that aspect of poker didn't appeal to them. They enjoyed the feeling of besting everyone else.

Slocum enjoyed the money, but he shared this drive to win with the two mine owners.

Slocum bet conservatively at first, then saw this wasn't working. He would lose the small pots far more than he won. After an hour, he was down several thousand dollars, all lost in bits and dabs. He was being nibbled to death by ducks. When he realized this, he changed his tactics.

"I'll raise you a thousand," Slocum said, bluffing with a bust hand.

"Indeed?" Hearst's eyebrow lifted slightly. He checked his hand. "I'll see that and buck you up another five hundred."

The weaselly man dropped out, saying, "Too rich for me."

Slocum looked at his worthless cards and nodded slightly. "Five thousand."

Hearst shook his head and threw his cards into the center of the table. "Your pot, Mr. Slocum."

Slocum kept from whopping with glee. He had recovered everything he had lost up to this point and was a thousand ahead. Slocum swallowed hard and stared at the money on the table. A thousand ahead. The numbers echoed in his head. He was winning and losing more money on each hand than he had seen in his entire life. And he liked it.

Most of all, he liked winning from George Hearst.

11

"You did well last night, John," Belle Flowers said.

"I won a few dollars," Slocum admitted. He hadn't counted the money he had given to Belle, but he thought he'd made close to five hundred off Hearst and the others when they had stopped play near two in the morning. The money was almost secondary to the feeling of winning. He had played some of the richest men in the country and had walked away from the table a winner.

"I ought to give it to you for such good work," she said, walking nervously around her parlor. Belle looked out through the lace curtains, as if she expected to see vigilantes riding up. It was almost with relief that she let the curtains fall back into place. Slocum wondered who she thought was out there.

"It was your stake. You ought to keep anything I made off it," said Slocum. He touched his pocket where the money she had paid him for posing as an engineer still rode. It wasn't as much as when he had received it, but it was still a sizable amount. Slocum had been without money most of his life, and now he had some—and the promise of a passel more.

He liked the notion of being so rich he could light his big, thick Cuban cigars with a twenty-dollar bill. That was about all a greenback was good for, unless you had enough of them.

He looked at her and tried to figure out what was going on. He had been as drunk with success as any liquor had ever made him when they left the Cassandra Club. He had thought Belle would offer to let him stay with her the night. She had been excited just being inside and rubbing shoulders with Hearst and his wealthy friends and business partners in the Consolidated Virginia Company. The money from the poker game was almost incidental to her, or so it seemed. That made Slocum all the more curious about her new scheme.

"Is he there?" Slocum asked. Belle jumped as if someone had stuck her with a pin.

"Who?"

"You look like someone scared of being followed. Is there something I ought to know?"

"That's none of your concern, John," she said, on edge. "Why don't you leave now? We have so much to do in the morning, and this evening has been a strain. It went well, but—" Belle looked on edge and glanced back toward the window, trying to see past the reflection and into the darkness toward Virginia City.

"All right. What time do you want me here in the morning?"

"Eight o'clock sharp. We have several mining properties to examine."

"Salt?" Slocum asked, pushing her just a mite. Belle was under pressure, and Slocum thought this might be the best time to see what he could learn. She just shook her head and waved him toward the door.

"Examine," she corrected sternly. "We are *not* doing anything illegal, John. You know that. It'll be just like tonight, with all the cards dealt and on the table. If someone makes a bet, he takes the risk. Now please, go."

Slocum picked up his fancy top hat and walked to the door. Belle was slow following him. He knew something was in the wind. He bid her good night and walked to the street. He paused a moment and saw her silhouette in the window, watching and waiting. He obliged her by walking down the street until he was out of sight, then he cut back and circled the house just in time to see a solitary rider dismounting at the kitchen porch.

As quiet as a shadow, Slocum crept back. He recognized the horse and knew who was inside. When he peeked through the window he saw a very drunk Reed Flowers arguing with Belle. The woman's voice carried shrilly as she berated him.

"They wanted money," she shouted.

"So?" Reed responded. He wobbled a mite, then caught himself on a chair and pulled himself around to sit heavily. "Ever'body wants money."

"It could blow the entire scam!" she shouted. "They wanted money you lost gambling."

"So? So I lost. I'm getting a third of everything. That's one helluva pile of money, sister dear. And I think you're holding out on me. Maybe you and this Slocum fellow you and Corey talk about all the time is cutting me out."

"Don't be ridiculous. That thousand dollars I·gave you was all we made off the first two mines. We just can't have you causing such a ruckus in town. Those men were the kind to break backs if they didn't collect. Can't you stop gambling, just for a week? That's all it will take for us to—"

"Whaddaya want me to do, Belle? Stop gamblin' and start whorin' with two-bit soiled doves?"

Slocum saw the woman's face turn livid with rage. She stamped her foot and her lips tightened to a thin, angry line, then spun and stormed from the room. The auburn-haired beauty was too furious to say a word. Reed sat in the chair for a moment, coughed, and forced himself to his feet. On shaky legs he came for the door. Slocum swung around and pressed himself flat against the wall.

Reed Flowers stumbled down the steps, muttering to himself, got onto his horse, almost fell from the saddle before finding the saddle horn to hang on to, then got the animal moving toward town. Slocum watched until the darkness swallowed them, then set out to find a place of his own to sleep for the night. The International was a fine hotel, but it cost too much.

With Reed Flowers drinking and gambling, and Belle worried that he would ruin her plans, everything might come unraveled soon. If it did, Slocum wanted to have as much money in his pocket as possible.

The Boiling Oil Mine was the fourth in a string of worthless holes they had looked at that morning and Slocum was getting tired. He didn't like riding in a buggy, even with Belle pressed close beside him. Preferring the freedom of his own horse had meant nothing to the woman. She insisted that he drive her around as they made their pointless examinations.

"There's not much inside to see," Slocum said, coming from the mine. At least Belle hadn't made him wear the fancy duds he'd worn to the opera. He had on his trail clothes, and the Colt Navy felt damned good swinging at his left hip. "The ore's been picked over pretty well."

"There are at least two veins of quartz running back into the mountainside," Belle said, looking over notes in a small book. She had entered her observations after every mine, but Slocum wasn't allowed to see what she was writing.

He was getting damned tired of being treated like a hired hand—or worse.

"The inside of the mine's hot." Slocum wiped sweat from his forehead. Many of the mines in the Comstock district filled with almost boiling hot water. Some deeper mines had a fifteen-minute work hour, letting the miners sit in front of fans blowing over ice. Anything less and dead men had to be lifted out of the shaft.

The best he could tell about the Boiling Oil Mine was that it angled down steeply. He'd heard Sutro wanted to drain the underground water but had little support from the other mine owners and partners in Consolidated Virginia. Slocum couldn't see anyone getting a speck of pay dirt out of this mine unless something was done to pump out the scalding water.

"The silver's not always where the most comfortable mining is, John. You know that."

"There's no silver here, Belle," he said firmly. "I'm not a mining engineer, but I don't have to be to see the mine's petered out. It might have given one man a decent living for a year or two, but no more. This is as worthless as tits on a boar hog."

"As you say, John, you are not a mining engineer," Belle said primly. She closed her notebook with a snap that sounded like a small caliber gunshot.

Slocum looked at her and started thinking. Greed was making him run a dangerous game. The thought of so much money being paid for the unproductive mine was like a carrot dangled in front of a mule. It kept him moving along, even if it was with real reluctance. But too much was happening to give Slocum a good feeling that he might walk away with any more money in his pocket than he had now.

Reed Flowers was the link in the devious chain that worried him most. Gambling and drinking attracted too much attention, even in a wide-open town like Virginia City. Slocum couldn't get the memory of the two miners out of his head. The mountain of a man wasn't going to stop looking for Flowers because the sheriff had thrown him in jail, and the smaller of the two might even have it in for Slocum now after the beating he had received. Such things didn't usually bother Slocum.

They did now. He didn't know what Belle's scheme was. The slightest upset in it might spell disaster for them all. Slocum shuddered, thinking of being thrown into the same cell with the two miners so intent on collecting Reed Flowers's gambling debt. He'd either have to kill them both the instant he was put into the cell or he would die as soon as he closed his eyes to sleep.

"What is it?" Slocum asked. "What are you doing to sell the Boiling Oil Mine to Hearst?"

"Perhaps it's not to Hearst," Belle said obliquely.

"Then why are you snorting up against his flank like a bitch in heat?" Slocum asked. He looked around the barren land. Small mountains of tailings scattered everywhere around the claim told of long, hard mining here. The quartz veins left inside were played out. Everything was barren, and he had the notion that Belle's morals weren't much different.

"The people Hearst knows have a great deal of money. The first dealings with him are our entry to their wallets." Belle looked smug, as if she had delivered lines read from her notebook. Slocum considered pulling the small book from her hands and reading the notes she had been making. It might give him a better idea what he was up against.

"Tell me what's going on," Slocum said. He had reached his decision. "How are you going to sell these worthless holes and get away with the money? And how long will it be until Hearst realizes the Silver Canary and the Spit Bucket aren't worth the money he paid for them?"

"You worry for no reason, John. Trust me. I know how these people think. We'll all be rich in another few days. A three-way split, just you and me and Corey."

Slocum started to ask if Belle intended to cut her brother out of the take, as she had on the first two mines. Slocum didn't think that Reed Flowers was doing a damned thing to help, but he couldn't be sure. He had to know where everything fit into the woman's scheme, and it was apparent she wasn't going to tell him.

He held back with his questions since it didn't seem likely Belle would tell him anything at all. The Cuckoo Clock and the Boiling Oil Mine were part of the new swindle, but who was getting robbed? Slocum was being paraded around so Hearst and the others at the Cassandra Club would get to know him. How was this important to Belle's plans?

"It's real nice up north this time of year," Slocum said. "No hot wind blowing down the canyon, kicking up dust, making your flesh turn to leather."

"What are you saying, John? I don't like the sound of this." Belle turned in the buggy seat and looked down at him. The light wind whipping along the ground caught her hair and turned it into a wild disarray that Slocum found entrancing. Belle's wide brown eyes were pools without limit, and he felt he could get lost in them. She was about the prettiest thing he'd ever seen.

He turned from her to keep from falling under her potent spell. If he stayed, he might end up rich. He might also end up in jail.

Oregon was nice in summer. Or even Idaho. It had been years since he'd stood on the banks of the Snake River and watched the rushing waters filled with fish jumping higher than his head. A man could forget all about the devious ways of the world, just for a while.

"You have a faraway look in your eye. John, only a few days. We'll be *rich*. Rich! Can you walk away from that? Can you walk away from me? I need you, John. I do."

She reached over and put her hand on his shoulder. Slocum looked back, knowing the risk he took. Her siren's call was so enticing. The money, the promises, Belle Flowers herself. He wanted it, but the risks were growing too fast for him. Slocum never thought of himself as a cautious man, but he only took risks he understood. Robbing a stagecoach with adequate planning was one thing. Going in blindly was something else.

What Belle asked of him was put on the blinders and follow her without question. He couldn't do it.

"I'm leaving," he said. "There's no reason for me to stay."

"The money, John. The thousand I gave you was just the start."

"Give me a third of what you made off the two mines you sold to Hearst. You said I helped you."

"No, John. You get an equal share of the next mines. You were well paid for the little work you did. Posing as an engineer wasn't hard. But this time, you'll have to do more."

"What else?" he asked. He was tired of her vagueness. She didn't even trust him enough to mention her brother and what role, if any, he had in selling the worthless mines.

"You'll find out soon. If I tell you before you need to know, everything might come apart. Please, John, trust me." Belle scooted to the edge of the buggy seat and swung around. The wind caught the edge of her skirt and lifted the cloth just enough to give Slocum a view of her fine, long legs.

Memories flooded back. He remembered what it was like to be between those legs, moving, responding, loving.

The memories were quickly banished when he felt Belle's hot lips crush against his. She slid down off the buggy and wrapped her arms around his neck to keep him close. Slocum knew she was trying to ensnare him even further in her web of sex. He knew and for the moment it didn't matter. They were on this barren hill, away from Virginia City and the schemes she spun so well, and he wanted one last time with the lovely woman. A parting present, he decided, was owed him.

"John, I need you for so much more than selling these dirty old mines. I need you to help me do everything. I want you so!" She kissed him again and this time he responded fully. His hands roamed up and down her firm body, finding the taut mounds of her breasts hidden under her blouse.

Squeezing hard on the tender breasts, he felt her body responding more and more. The tight points cresting her breasts pumped full of aroused blood and turned into tiny knives jabbing hard into his chest. He took her left breast and massaged it, kneading the flesh, pressing his thumb into the nipple. Through it he felt the throbbing of her heart. This wasn't feigned. She wanted him. She wanted him and there was no concealing it.

"Here, John, now. I'm sorry I was so distracted last night. You should have stayed." Belle lifted her leg and wrapped it around his waist. She tensed her muscles and pulled herself even closer. Then she began rubbing up and down.

Slocum stiffened painfully. He was trapped in his canvas pants and couldn't get out—until Belle started helping him.

"John, now, I need you now." She fumbled with the balky buttons holding his fly closed. He moaned as she worked eagerly to free him, her hand brushing against him and making him feel even more trapped. When he snapped out, erect and ready, it was almost as much of a relief as finishing with the lovely auburn-haired woman would be.

"Belle," he started, but she silenced him with kisses. Moving closer, he slid his hands under her rounded buttocks. He lifted so that both her feet were off the ground. Like a monkey climbing a tree, Belle circled his body, clinging fiercely to him.

Both her legs circled his waist. She levered herself up and then down. Slocum was startled to find she wasn't wearing anything under her dress. The purpled tip of his manhood brushed across her moistened nether lips, then plunged deep into her body. Slocum's knees almost buckled as she surrounded him totally.

Kissing all over his face and neck, her arms around his body, her long, strong legs gripping his waist and the firmness enveloping his length made him wobble.

Slocum turned and braced himself against the buggy. The horse snorted and tried to shy. Slocum ignored it as Belle began moving up and down, using her thighs and arms to propel herself. He gasped with every twitch of her hips. He moaned when she began thrashing about faster, harder. And he tried to hold back the fiery tide building in his balls when she rushed down around him like a collapsing mine shaft.

He tried and failed. The fierce flow erupted from him like a spewing volcano.

Belle shrieked out like a howling coyote as the stark power of the lovemaking seized her. She tossed back her head and whipped her long auburn hair around like a cavalry troop's unfurled victory banner. Then she rocked forward again, still clinging hard to Slocum and put her head on his shoulder.

"John, oh, John, so nice. You're so *good.*"

Slocum was turning limp, but he held on to Belle for several minutes until his aching muscles cramped. He whirled her around and got her feet under her before stepping back. Her skirt was wrinkled where she had hiked it up and her blouse had dirty handprints on it where he had fondled her breasts.

And her face glowed. Belle Flowers was a gorgeous woman, but now she looked more beautiful than any mortal ever had.

"You won't leave me, will you, John?" she asked in a tiny voice, as if she were afraid of his answer. "I need you, and it's not just because we'll both be rich in a few days. I need more than just money." She moved closer and kissed him gently.

If she had kissed him with the passion that had blasted forth before, Slocum might have thought she was coldly using sex to hold him. Now he wasn't sure—and in that uncertainty might lie the seeds of his own destruction.

He heard himself answering, as if from a thousand miles off, "I'll stay, Belle. For a few more days."

Her smile was worth any risk.

12

Slocum left Belle at her house, then turned toward town downslope from Gold Hill. Virginia City in the middle of the afternoon was almost sedate. The more raucous whorehouses were silent, and the melodian shows weren't slated to open for several more hours. In a way, Slocum appreciated the quiet.

He went into the Howling Wilderness for a drink. Slocum sat in a corner and nursed his whiskey as he thought hard. It was foolish of him to stay if Belle didn't trust him enough to tell him what was going on. She had something in the works that didn't include him. He saw it and knew she wasn't a small-time operator. The huge amount of money she had swindled from George Hearst proved that.

But what was the woman up to? And where did Slocum fit in?

He worried on that score. He ought to cover his own ass in some way, but he didn't know how. All he could do was keep his horse rested and ready for a quick run out of the district, even if a posse came after him. Slocum swallowed the fiery liquor and realized even such speed might not be good enough if he angered Hearst.

The mining magnate had a reach far exceeding the Comstock. Pinkertons might be sent after Slocum if this deal turned sour, or Hearst might go so far as to hire a small army of bounty hunters. If the swindle was big enough, what was a few extra thousand dollars to a man involved with the Consolidated Virginia Company and the resources hinted at by looking at a roster of the company's owners?

Slocum had to talk with Hearst again and see if he had alerted the man. Slocum was torn about this tactic. If he warned Hearst away from Belle's swindle, he might cause the trouble he sought to avoid. But if Reed Flowers jinxed the swindle, Slocum needed a way out. It might not be enough hinting to Hearst that he was opening a can of worms, but it'd be better than nothing.

Slocum sipped his drink and considered just leaving Virginia City again.

Huge piles of money. Belle. And Corey.

Those three things kept coming back to haunt him. How many men were given the chance he need only sit back and take? His thoughts turned to how he should spend the money he'd get off the scam.

In the middle of his daydream, he heard three men enter the saloon and ask the barkeep where he was. The sound of his name brought Slocum around. He turned slightly in his chair, his hand reaching to his cross-draw holster and the leather thong holding the hammer of his six-shooter. He slipped it off and got ready for trouble.

He relaxed a mite when he saw two of the three men were Hearst's agents. The men had been bamboozled by the Flowers sisters, but Slocum didn't think they were likely to raise much of a ruckus over it. Somehow, Belle or Corey had altered the assay reports coming back on ore taken from the Spit Bucket Mine and the Silver Canary. It might look as if the two were out to swindle Hearst, but Slocum thought they could talk their way out of any trouble.

Hell, it might be months before Hearst got around to sending miners into the mines to reap his fabulous rewards. It was enough to make Slocum smile. Hearst wasn't going to end up with nothing, but it might as well be nothing for the price he paid. He'd be lucky to get back a nickel on every dollar spent.

"Howdy, gents," Slocum greeted as the men came over. The two agents weren't dangerous. The third man with them had the look of a gun slick about him. Slocum gave him a quick once over and saw a man ready to fight and kill. This put him on edge. Something had gone wrong.

"Don't go doin' it, Mr. Slocum," Hanrahan said.

"We got ways to stop you," piped up the other. He licked dried lips and glanced over to the hired gun.

Slocum straightened a little in the chair, getting his right hand a bit closer to the ebony handle of his Colt Navy. The man with Hearst's flunkies twitched slightly, as if he wanted to end this now with a single slug through Slocum's head.

"Something's eating you," Slocum said. "Why not just come on out and say it?"

"We work for Consolidated Virginia Company," Hanrahan said.

"Tell me something I don't know," Slocum said, cutting him off. He had thought the men worked for Hearst personally, but it didn't matter that much. Hearst and Consolidated Virginia had similar goals. If one prospered, so did the other. The partners in the mining conglomerate were all filthy rich and content to let Hearst do what he wanted—as long as it made them money.

Slocum began to wonder if he had bitten off more than he could chew. Hearst was one tough hombre, but he might be up against all Consolidated Virginia's owners.

"Why don't you just own up to what you're doing, Slocum?" demanded the gunman. His hand twitched again. Slocum had seen men like this before. If the trigger finger curled just a tad more, the man would go for iron. Slocum had to be dragging his own six-gun out before that happened or he wouldn't have a chance.

"What am I doing?" Slocum asked. "And what call do you have sticking your nose in my business?" Slocum felt his heart pounding faster when he saw the gunfighter's shoulders pull back. The man was getting ready to draw. The first shot would determine who lived and who died.

Slocum curled his foot around the table leg, ready to kick out and send the table spinning toward the trio. This would give him precious seconds to get off a round or two.

"I'm foreman for Consolidated Virginia," the gunfighter said. "It's my call to—"

"Goddammit, Slocum, you son of a bitch!" came the roar from across the room. The Howling Wilderness's front doors slammed open and glass broke, tinkling noisily to the floor. "You can't go tellin' lies like you been doin'!"

Slocum was as startled by the intrusion as the three Consolidated Virginia men. Reed Flowers stood in the door, his face fiery red in anger. His chest heaved and he carried an ax handle. He lifted and dropped it into his left palm. The smacking noise silenced those in the saloon who hadn't quieted when he slammed through the doors.

"You miserable sidewinder. You lyin' son of a bitch!" Flowers rushed forward, cocking his ax handle behind him as he ran.

Slocum looked from the charging Reed Flowers to the gunman standing with the Consolidated Virginia agents. The gun slick didn't look to be the problem Flowers was—and Slocum didn't have a clue what brought on this attack.

He stood, straightening his leg as he did so. This caused the table to spin around, ramming square into Flowers's legs. The man tumbled over the table. Slocum drew with a smooth movement and pulled back the hammer. In a low, deadly voice, he said, "If you want to keep on living, you'll turn around and get the hell out of here. I don't want to see you again."

Slocum had reached a decision unconsciously. He had been lying to himself trying to find reasons to stay and rake in the big money Belle promised. The three men from Consolidated Virginia didn't much bother him, but they did make him wonder what was going on. And now Reed Flowers came rushing in, hellbent to part Slocum's hair with the wood stave.

This was the straw that broke the camel's back. Slocum saw no reason to stay in the Comstock district.

"You can't go tellin' lies!" raved Flowers, struggling to get off the table. Slocum kicked the table again and unbalanced the furious man again. Flowers tumbled forward, but this time he rolled off and landed on the floor. Pushing up from hands and knees, he stood. The ax handle swung viciously in front of him.

Slocum considered ending it there. A single slug would settle Flowers's hash. But he was all too aware of the three men at the side of the room. He saw the gunman's finger curling and his hand twitching. He wanted an excuse to kill Slocum.

Against his better instincts, Slocum holstered his Colt Navy and swung to face Flowers. The man screamed again, attacked with the ax handle held high—and ended up flat on his back. Slocum caught his wrist, deflected the swing, and connected to the man's belly with a short, hard right. Slocum's fist sank to the wrist in soft flesh. He was sorry he couldn't have put more power behind the punch.

Flowers was still conscious and gasping for breath. Slocum needed him out of the fight to tend to the three now standing behind him. He kicked out, trying to land the blow on Flowers's chin. Slocum missed by less than an inch.

"You won't get away with it," Flowers mumbled, getting to his feet and holding his jaw. Slocum took a deep breath, gauged his distance, and swung again. The shock of hitting bone rattled all the way up into his left shoulder, numbing his arm. Flowers staggered and went down, clutching his chest. Slocum's aim had been just a tad off. He had aimed for the man's solar plexus and had hit a rib.

"What the hell's this about?" Slocum demanded. He saw that Flowers wasn't going to give up easily. Maybe he could talk him out of this crazy fight.

"You know. You been goin' around town lyin' about how much silver's in those mines. There're tons of silver in there! The Cuckoo Clock'll give up fifteen thousand dollars a week!" Reed Flowers got his feet under him and wobbled around. Slocum considered hitting him again. He didn't have to. Flowers's legs gave out and he just sat down, holding his head and protesting Slocum's lies.

Slocum turned to the three from the Consolidated Virginia Company and widened his stance. The gunman was ready to go for his six-shooter. Slocum was all keyed up and all he wanted to do was take a few minutes to settle down, but he'd draw if he had to defend himself. His hands hurt from the punches he had landed, but he had fought it out like this before and hadn't had any trouble holding his Colt or aiming accurately. And speed? He was ready.

His attitude communicated to the two agents with the gunman. One put his hand on the man's arm, only to have it shrugged off. If Slocum had wanted to shoot it out, this would have been his cue. The gunfighter's attention was off his target, just for a split second. Slocum could have had him cold.

But he held back. He wasn't inclined to leave dead bodies behind. Corpses tended to have brothers and friends. And Slocum was more curious as to what brought all this down around his ears.

"You're lying," gasped out Reed Flowers. "There *is* silver in that mine. In all of them!"

Slocum listened for any sound that Flowers was coming up behind him, but the fight had gone out of him. All he was doing now was mewling sickly and complaining about Slocum badmouthing the quality of the mines.

"What do you gents really want?" Slocum asked. He kept his eyes fixed on the gunman's belly. It wasn't possible for a man to draw without tensing up just a mite. Slocum had seen stone killers whose eyes never showed as much as a flicker of emotion as they drew and killed. He had learned a long time back that muscles betrayed more men than their eyes.

"You know what's riling us," the gunman said. "You steer clear of those mines. Don't go nosin' around them. They're our concern." The man's jaw tensed and he added, "They're *my* concern."

"Slade, the sheriff," whispered Hanrahan. "At the door."

Slocum heard others in the saloon yelling out to the law what had gone on. Reed Flowers was crawling on his hands and knees toward the door. The sheriff was likely to let him leave since there wasn't any sign of blood. A man getting busted up in a bar fight wasn't hardly cause to send anyone to jail. But the two faced off at the rear of the saloon might give him another view on the matter.

"You've been warned, Slocum. You butt out. If I see you around any of those mines, you're gonna be buzzard bait." Slade relaxed just enough for Slocum to know the gunman wasn't going to draw on him. The other two agents bustled him from the Howling Wilderness, pushing past the sheriff. The lawman turned and watched them go, then came over.

"What's got into you, mister? That's Luke Slade, foreman at—"

"Consolidated Virginia," Slocum finished for him. "He introduced himself."

"Then you know that the only reason he's in Virginia City is to take care of labor problems. Consolidated Virginia doesn't want any strikes slowing the silver production."

"Reckon they wouldn't like that." Slocum said, picking up his hat and getting it settled on his head. He wondered what the hell this dust-up had been about. But it didn't matter. In the morning he'd ride north and be out of Virginia City before most folks finished breakfast.

13

His horse neighed and woke Slocum just before dawn. He shivered and pulled his blanket up around his shoulders. He groaned when the horse neighed again. The stableboy was supposed to feed and tend to the gelding, but Slocum was here and the boy wasn't. He rolled onto his back and stared up at the wood roof on the stable.

Virginia City was one hell of a strange city. He could have spent another hundred dollars and stayed in the International—and the notion had appealed to him. It could have been a last hurrah, one last glimpse of the high life he was giving up. But the hotel was booked solid for the next month. A passel of mine owners had come into town early yesterday, most of them having something to do with Consolidated Virginia or its rival, the Consolidated California Company.

Staying in a lesser, cheaper hotel would have been fine, but they were all filled, too. Slocum had started his hunt for lodging too late. Boom towns tended to overdo everything. The hint of new discoveries out in the Comstock Lode had brought in droves of new miners to try their luck. Most were too young to have taken part in the '49 gold rush in

117

California or even the '69 rush here in the Comstock. They had the money to keep them going a few weeks, and they were eager to lose it digging in worthless rock.

Until the prospectors did, the hotels would be filled until their brick walls bulged—and John Slocum would sleep with his horse, although he had purt' near eight hundred dollars wadded up in his shirt pocket.

He might have gone to Belle and asked to sleep up there on Gold Hill. If nothing more than to keep him around, Belle and Corey would have agreed to him sleeping in the huge house. But he was damned if he'd go near either of them again. They were lovely but played a hand he didn't understand. Slocum didn't mind playing and losing, but he had to know the rules and stand some small chance of winning.

"So much money," he said aloud. His horse didn't care. It wanted hay. "They rooked Hearst out of more than a third of a million dollars, and still they want more." He brushed the straw off his clothes and blanket and got down to work. Slocum thought hard as he finished brushing the horse.

He wondered if the men pouring into Virginia City had something to do with Belle's scheme to sell the Cuckoo Clock Mine. She had gone to great lengths salting the mine and dumping tons of silver-rich ore at the base of the hill. It might take a meeting of the board of directors of Consolidated Virginia before they could pony up more money to buy the bogus claim.

Slocum chuckled to himself, then said to his gelding, "I wonder if Hearst even told the others in the company he bought the Spit Bucket and the Silver Canary? He might be double-dealing his own partners."

He tried to work out what it all meant and finally gave up. Belle and Hearst worked at levels too complex for him to understand. He had a goodly sum, even if it was in greenbacks, riding in his poke. It was time to move on and to hell with Reed Flowers, Hearst and the Consolidated Virginia Company, Luke Slade, and even Belle and Corey.

Slocum mounted, then sat for a moment. He had to give one last try to letting Hearst know his agents might be doing him wrong. The thought of the two terrified mice that had accompanied Slade the night before rankled. For all Slocum knew, Hearst was being fleeced by his own men. He didn't owe the mining magnate anything, but it didn't hurt to talk to him one last time.

He dismounted and walked his horse out and down the street toward Hearst's office. To his surprise, the mine owner was already at work. His secretary hadn't shown up yet, so Slocum walked in and rapped on the office door. Hearst looked up, his face almost completely hidden by the thick blue plumes of smoke from his fat cigar.

"Slocum, didn't expect to see you so early. Come in, come in."

Slocum sat in the chair to one side of the desk and waited a few seconds for Hearst to finish the work that so engrossed him.

"Got so much paperwork to do, it hardly seems worth it. That's a penalty for being rich, eh?" Hearst signed the bottom of one page with a flourish and sat back, puffing like a steam engine on his stogie. "I wanted to talk to you about that set-to last night."

It surprised Slocum that Hearst would even mention sending his bulldog over. Then he thought a mite on it and wasn't sure why anything ought to astound him.

"Slade wasn't much of a bother," Slocum said.

"You're about the only man in these parts who'd say that. He's one tough hombre. Chews nails and spits tacks. I like that. Hell, I *need* that. Those pantywaist miners are always prattling about unions and going on strike, just to get out of working an honest day. Can't have another Battle Mountain here, no, sir."

"Did you check the assay on the two mines?" Slocum asked. He felt the bottoms of his feet beginning to itch. It was time for him to be traveling on. He had no call sitting and making small talk with George Hearst.

"No need. The original assay was good. You keep harping on those two mines." Hearst got a shrewd look in his eyes. "Why's that?"

"Hate to see a man done out of his money. If you're happy with the work your agents are doing, I've got nothing more to say."

"Sit down." Hearst barked it out, more of a command than a request. Slocum paused, wondering if he ought to keep going. He could be in Nevada City in a day or two.

"I've said my piece. There's not much more I can tell you."

"The Cuckoo Clock Mine. You think it's played out, don't you?"

Slocum shrugged. If Hearst wouldn't listen to him about mines he'd already paid for, he wasn't likely to pay heed to warnings about salting on a third mine.

"It's a gamble, I admit it, but less of one than playing the stock market." Hearst stubbed out his cigar and immediately cut and lit another. "You play the market, Slocum? Didn't think so. You're more comfortable facing a man when you gamble."

Slocum had nothing to say. He wondered where this was heading. He wanted to hit the trail as soon as he could.

"Consolidated Virginia trades on the San Francisco exchange. Some days it goes as high as five hundred dollars a share. It's been soaring since news of the new silver strikes hit."

"How many shares do you own?" Slocum asked.

Hearst laughed. "I like you, Slocum. You've got guts. Not many have that. They come in here and start stuttering, as if I'm the Lord God on high. Hell, I'll tell you. I own ten thousand shares. And that's only a fraction of what I have. My son is starting a newspaper over in San Francisco with my money, I own dozens of gold and silver mines that have nothing to do with Consolidated Virginia, then there's the brewery down the street. I own a great deal, and control even more. Money is power, Slocum."

Slocum had seen no fewer than five breweries feeding a hundred saloons. That might be where the real money was in Virginia City, now that most of the silver and gold had been mined. Hearst wasn't going to tell him how many of the saloons he owned, not that it was any of his business. He had simply asked to give himself time to think.

Hearst helped him along by rattling on about all he controlled in Virginia City.

"I own part of the International Hotel. I could go on, but why bother? You got your horse outside, Slocum?"

"I was riding out," Slocum admitted.

"Good. Let's take a little trip. Not a long one. Maybe an hour. It'll be worth your time." Hearst heaved his bulk from the chair and puffed across the room, leaving behind a cloying fog of cigar smoke. Slocum had no reason to go with Hearst. Then again, he didn't have any reason not to. He got outside in time to see Hearst climbing into a buckboard. It was hardly the kind of transportation Slocum expected of such a wealthy man.

"You can ride with me or get on that nag of yours. Your choice, Slocum." Hearst snapped the reins and got his team moving. Both horses strained, although the buckboard was empty of anything except Hearst's bulk. Slocum wondered if any horse, even a Percheron, would hold the huge man.

Slocum caught up and trotted alongside the wagon. Hearst still puffed, but the smoke was pulled away by the strong wind blowing down the canyon. The Washoe Zephyr was something else Slocum wouldn't miss much. Hot, dry, it reminded him of bleached bones and lonely graveyards.

"See yonder?" called Hearst, pointing by lifting his chin to the right. "That's the Union Mine. And not far from it is the Sierra Nevada. Two of the richest mines in the whole Comstock. I swear the mother lode runs smack through both claims."

"Yours?"

"Part of the Consolidated Virginia Company holdings," Hearst said. "Sutro's been ragging on us to pump the water from the mines. You know about that, don't you? Heard tell you were over at the Boiling Oil Mine giving it the once over."

"You think pumping out the hot water's all it'd take to open up a new boom?" Slocum shook his head. "I don't know much about these things, but those mines aren't worth the money you're paying."

"Who's to say, Slocum? You're a hotshot mining engineer, but the assays don't lie. You're making a mistake."

"Might be," Slocum allowed, "but I don't think so. Not this time." He rode along in silence for a spell, then asked, "Why are you showing me those mines? Seeing ones that are fabulously rich isn't going to change my mind."

"Didn't intend it to. Turn around, head back to town." Hearst wheeled his wagon in a wide circle. Slocum hesitated, then rode back toward Virginia City with Hearst.

"Why are we out here?" Slocum repeated.

"Isn't it obvious?" Hearst snorted, then spat, sending the butt of his cigar in a high arc. "I'm showing you Consolidated Virginia's best property, telling you some of the problems. That boiling water Adolf is always going on about is a damned nuisance. Cuts down on mine production something fierce."

Slocum took a second to realize Hearst meant Adolf Sutro. He wasn't used to millionaires being referred to by their first names. And he still didn't know what Hearst was getting at.

"You offering me a job?" Slocum was startled at the idea. Hearst had no reason in the world to open a position for him. The mine owner had spent most of the morning driving home the point that Slocum was probably wrong in his evaluation of the Flowers's mines. Why hire someone who told you what a waste of money the mines were?

"Of course I am. You're nobody's fool. I'll pay you two hundred a week. That's not great money in Virginia City, but it's more than you'd likely see staying with Belle Flowers."

"What job?" Slocum still couldn't believe this. He was being offered twice what Belle had given him to pretend to be her foreman.

"You go around to the mines and check on safety. You report straight back to me."

"Not to Luke Slade?"

This brought Hearst around. His eyes bored into Slocum's green ones. "There are people in Consolidated Virginia I didn't hire. Slade is one of them. I'm a shareholder and run most things."

"But not all. The other partners insisted on hiring him?"

"Slade is useful in labor negotiations," Hearst said. "I don't credit him with the sense God gave a goose. You've got a wit, and you must know how to use that hogleg hanging at your side. That's a rare combination in any man. I want you on my side."

"For how long? How long would I be on the company payroll?"

Hearst laughed heartily. "I knew you were shrewd, Slocum. Let's ride to the Cassandra Club and discuss it over lunch. I've been up for hours and have worked up a powerful appetite."

Slocum and Hearst said nothing during the fifteen-minute ride to the posh club. In daylight it looked even more impressive than it had at night. Hearst dropped off the wagon with a heavy thud and bustled up the marble steps. Slocum was slower to follow. The same liveried doorman eyed him in the same way, his gaze falling to Slocum's side arm. Slocum handed it over without comment.

"There's my private dining room, Slocum. I've taken the liberty of ordering for us. A little Cornish game hen is always good. And wine from France."

Slocum sat on the edge of the hand-carved wood chair, not even moving the chair closer, afraid he might crush something that wobbled so precariously under him. Hearst had no compunction about dropping into his chair. It creaked and protested the sudden weight on it but held. Slocum relaxed and leaned back to let the waiter serve him some wine in a crystal goblet. He tasted it.

"Fine stuff, isn't it, Slocum?" demanded Hearst. "I had it shipped around the Cape from France."

"Don't have much call to drink wine," Slocum said. "I can say it's been a while since anything this smooth slid down my gullet."

Hearst downed his wine in a single gulp and attacked the game hen on the plate in front of him with gusto. It took only minutes for him to finish the first. Four hens later, he wiped greasy fingers on a white linen napkin and leaned back. Slocum had eaten more slowly, still not sure why he was even here.

"So? Do you want the job?" asked Hearst.

"All I do is check the timbers, see to working conditions, be sure the stopes are being drilled properly?"

"It's a necessary job," Hearst said. "And Sutro might like your advice on draining the water. He's going to tunnel through a mountain or some such nonsense to get rid of it."

"For as long as a month?"

Hearst laughed again. "There'll be a fine bonus for you at the end of every month. And club privileges. You can come here and put whatever you want on the company account."

"Don't reckon I'd even want to go see the mines if I had this to look forward to." Slocum wiped the grease off his lips and dropped the napkin beside his fine bone china plate. The silent waiter removed it and replaced it with something dark, red, and frozen.

"Sherbet," Hearst said. "Can't get enough of it. Made from strawberries and ice and who knows what else?" He devoured his helping. A second serving appeared as if by magic. Slocum stopped eating his when his temples began to ache.

"What about Slade?"

"You and Slade won't cross trails. I swear, you ask more questions than any other man I ever tried to hire. You'd think you were the only engineer in the district." Hearst leaned forward, his elbows on the table. "I know good men when I see them. Take the job, Slocum."

This came out with more than a hint of threat wrapped around it. Hearst was a man used to getting what he wanted and nobody stopped him—not for long.

"The offer's attractive, Mr. Hearst," Slocum said. "Let me think on it and give you my decision by this afternoon."

Hearst's eyebrows shot up. He hadn't thought Slocum would refuse. Slocum waited just long enough to watch the astonishment fade. Hearst waved him off, starting in on a third helping of the sherbet.

14

Slocum left the Cassandra Club, an uneasy sensation gnawing away at his innards. He took his Colt Navy back from the doorman and cinched it up tight around his waist. He paused for a moment, wondering if he should go back and talk to Hearst a last time to make the man understand that Belle and Corey were playing him for a fool. Slocum decided against it. Hearst wasn't the kind who thought anyone could snooker him, much less two lovely women.

The uneasiness grew when Slocum stepped out into the bright Nevada sunlight. The other times he had felt this sensation meant he was being trailed. Twice in the past year he had gotten away from Apaches hot for his scalp by heeding this sensation. He had never seen the war parties as he had dodged across the New Mexico deserts on his way to Nevada, but he knew they'd been there, he had *felt* them behind him.

He mounted his gelding, using this opportunity to look around. He didn't see anyone obviously watching him. Rather than relieving him, this made the uncanny intuition all the stronger. He was being watched and whoever it was didn't want to be seen. Someone knew he had eaten lunch with George Hearst. That meant he was being followed by someone working for Consolidated Virginia.

What more did they want from him?

Slocum turned toward the outskirts of Virginia City but found himself slowly spiraling back into town, riding in circles, moving to keep whoever followed him off guard and guessing where he went. They must want to know where he was heading. If he just rode north out of town as he had intended, trailing him would be easy. And that wasn't what Slocum wanted. He needed to know how dangerous his unseen watchers were before leaving.

Riding aimlessly up and down Virginia City's crowded, quartz-ore-covered streets, Slocum thought hard about Hearst's offer. The mine owner wanted to hire Slocum away from Belle, that much was clear. What did Hearst think he could do for him that he wasn't getting from any of a dozen other men? Or was he just trying to keep Slocum from giving Belle any help?

And Hearst had to know Belle had offered him a hundred a week to be her foreman, but he didn't know she had paid him a thousand dollars to pose as a mining engineer. Hearst thought Slocum was trained in drilling, support timbers, and all the rest of the dark, arcane arts known only to men who lived their lives—and sometimes lost their lives—underground.

Or did he? Maybe he knew Slocum's background better than Belle and just wanted a possible problem solved before he dickered with the Flowers sisters for the Cuckoo Clock and the Boiling Oil mines. Luke Slade had the look of a quick hand to him, but Slocum was better. He knew it and he thought Hearst did, too.

Slocum held his head. His temples still ached from eating the sherbet too fast, and trying to sort through the complicated warp and woof of Belle's plot was giving him an even bigger headache.

Slocum didn't know why he felt any obligation at all to warn Hearst when the man obviously didn't care. Or he might be playing a game of his own. He wasn't stupid, even if he did have money to burn.

Turning sharply, Slocum caught sight of sunlight glinting off metal. The man trailing him had finally made a mistake—and Slocum thought he knew who it was. He rode a ways farther along A Street, made as if going to Gold Hill and Belle's house, then cut down a ravine and dismounted. He tethered his horse and scrambled back up the shale slope in time to drop on his belly.

The man rode by, sitting awkwardly astride his horse as if he didn't do much riding. He had to pull even with Slocum's hiding place before he was recognizable.

It was Sam Hanrahan, one of Hearst's agents. He craned his neck to see where Slocum had gone. Slocum considered calling out to him and scaring him out of a year's growth, then held back. Better to watch and wait and see what happened.

Slocum was now the tracker and knew his quarry.

Hanrahan looked puzzled at Slocum's sudden disappearance, then directed his gaze up Gold Hill toward Belle's house. Hanrahan spurred his horse in that direction. Slocum watched carefully. Hanrahan rode past the house, reached the end of the street, and rode back, never taking his eyes off the front of the house. As he came back, a look of disgust etched his face.

Slocum heard him grumble as he urged his horse to greater speed. Hanrahan wasn't pleased he had let Slocum get away, and it seemed as if he had other business to attend to before he could rest. The Consolidated Virginia agent trotted off, forcing Slocum to make a decision.

Go or stay.

He hardly thought about it as he skidded down the hillside and jumped into the saddle. Curiosity was as bad a vice as greed or letting his balls do his thinking for him. But Slocum was hit from all sides by puzzles. Belle and Corey, Hearst and the money, the scheme to sell the Cuckoo Clock and the Boiling Oil mines, the warning Reed Flowers had given him for no apparent reason—and the Consolidated Virginia agents in the saloon—all fed his desire to stick it out.

"What's another day or two, old friend?" he asked the gelding as he guided the horse along Virginia City's streets until he caught sight of Hanrahan. The horse snorted in disgust, as if telling Slocum exactly what it thought.

Hanrahan stopped and talked with the other agent, who checked his watch, then mounted his horse. The pair rode out of town, heading toward the Cuckoo Clock Mine. Slocum hung back, knowing where they went. A few miles outside town, he left the road and cut across the rugged country, approaching the mine from downslope. He stood a better chance of being seen as he got closer, but from the nervous way Hanrahan and his friend kept glancing over their shoulders made him think this was really the safer route.

He left his horse near the salted tailings where he hoped it wouldn't be noticed, then wound back and forth up the trail until he heard voices above him. Slocum ducked down. He saw Belle and Corey standing at the top of the trail. They were arguing, as they seemed to do when no one was around to see.

"It's time to spring the trap," Corey insisted. "He's hooked."

"Slocum's no fool—don't underestimate him," Belle snapped. "We've planned this for months. If we hurry it, we might lose everything."

"If we don't," Corey shot back, "we might end up in jail. We've got enough money now. Let's call this off and just hightail it."

"No!" Belle was adamant.

"Oh, you want to pay off our dear brother's debts? Remember how unpleasant it was the night you and Slocum went to the opera? Running headlong into two men Reed owes gambling debts to almost ruined everything."

"We can pull this off if we don't get spooked. I want to—" She bit off her words as the pounding of horses' hooves sounded. Both women turned away from the path.

Slocum relaxed a tad, then began a sneak up the hill to a spot where he could see what was happening.

Hanrahan and the other agent were dismounting. Slocum settled down, out of sight behind a rusted stack of machinery. He thought he might finally discover what was going on.

"Sam, so good to see you again!" Belle threw her arms around Hanrahan's neck and kissed him firmly.

Hanrahan pushed her back. The other man stepped away when Corey tried to greet him the same way.

"You lied to us," Hanrahan accused. "You did something to those assay reports we showed you."

"Why, Sam, whatever are you saying?" Belle fluttered her eyelashes at him and put on the "poor li'l ole me" look. "Mr. Hearst bought those two mines all on his own."

"Somebody's been spreading rumors that the Silver Canary and the Spit Bucket are the new Comstock Lode stars," the second man said. "There's not much silver left in either."

"I'm sure Mr. Hearst knows his own mind."

"You doctored the assay reports. That's what it was," Hanrahan said, sticking to his guns. He put balled hands on his hips and looked as if he wanted to hit Belle. She didn't give any indication she noticed anything was wrong.

"You handed Mr. Hearst the reports. However could we have changed them?" she asked, batting her eyelashes some more.

"That night, when we, you, the two of us—" Hanrahan sputtered, then shook his head. "When Hearst finds there's nothing worth three hundred fifty thousand dollars in those mines, he'll hand us our heads."

The other agent shuddered visibly and said, "Hearst won't do it. He'll have Slade do it. I heard tell he was tortured by the Crow for almost a month and lived to brag on it. The things he knows, the things that were done to him he can do to us."

"You men do worry so," cooed Corey. "We didn't bring

you out here to talk about torture and other . . . repulsive things." Corey went to the Consolidated Virginia agent and put her hand on his shoulder. "I'm sure we can find more interesting topics, can't we?"

"We have to look over the mine," Hanrahan said firmly. "That's what Hearst pays us for."

"And you do it so well, too," Belle said. "He's made half a dozen fortunes off your talents." She got a mock confused look on her face as she added, "Are you sharing in his good fortune? The good fortune you've brought him?"

"He doesn't pay us shit," the second agent said.

Hanrahan silenced his partner with a hard look. "We got jobs. We have to do them."

"Why, Sam, of course you do," said Belle. "Do get on with it. The Cuckoo Clock is a fine property. And when you finish here, we can ride to the Boiling Oil Mine and three others. The entire package is easily worth a million dollars."

"If this one ain't worth cold spit, we won't bother with the others," Hanrahan said sharply.

"What a strange attitude to take, Sam," Belle said. "We might be wrong about how much silver is left in the Cuckoo Clock. Maybe it's not as much as we think, but the Boiling Oil and the others are different mines. They are—"

"I checked the records, Belle," Hanrahan said, cutting her off. "The Cuckoo Clock was the richest of the lot. If we don't find enough silver inside to justify the purchase, there's no point in wasting more time."

"Belle," said Corey, "perhaps we should approach the *other* interested party. I don't think Mr. Hanrahan is going to present our properties in the proper light to Mr. Hearst."

"What other buyer?" demanded Hanrahan. He snorted in disgust when the women only smiled sweetly. He motioned to his partner, and they went into the Cuckoo Clock's main tunnel.

"We've got to get them to check the tailings, Belle," said Corey. "We spent damned near ten thousand dollars getting that high-grade ore moved in from the Crown Point. I don't want to waste the money."

"It's not wasted," Belle said. "Everything is going along just fine."

Slocum settled down and strained to hear what else Belle and Corey were saying, but the women lowered their voices and whispered. In less than ten minutes, Hanrahan and the other man came from the mine. Hanrahan's face was flushed and the set of his body told he had discovered how Reed Flowers had salted the mine.

"Sam, you finished your examination quickly. We—"

"Salted, Belle, the goddamn mine's been salted. I even found the shotgun shell on the floor."

"Sam, I don't know what you're saying. Check the tailings. I've been told the debris from the Cuckoo Clock is worth more than the blue dirt from other mines."

"You're trying to swindle Consolidated Virginia just like you did before. If Hearst gives you so much as a plugged nickel for this mine, it'll be over my dead body." Hanrahan motioned to his friend to leave. They turned. Belle and Corey rushed forward, protesting loudly.

"You've got this all wrong, Sam. I don't know anything about salting. The mine's good. It's worth the money I'm asking. It's worth more!"

"Only a quarter million," Corey said. "Take an option on the other mines, but you have to buy the Cuckoo Clock!"

"I've heard and seen about all I need," Hanrahan said. "Count on me telling Hearst about it." The set to his body and his tone told Slocum the report wasn't going to be favorable for the Flowers sisters.

"And about how you let doctored assay reports on the Silver Canary and the Spit Bucket get into his hands?" Belle asked.

"I'll take my chances on that. Better to have Hearst lose a few hundred thousand than a million." Hanrahan mounted clumsily and turned away from Belle and Corey. His partner put spurs to his horse's flanks and raced off ahead of Hanrahan, as if he didn't trust himself to stay and listen to the women's excuses.

"Sam—" Belle started. Corey grabbed her arm and stopped her from going after the man.

"Never mind him now," Corey said. "How are we going to handle this?"

Slocum didn't hear Belle's reply. Both women were turned away from him so he couldn't see their faces. He considered going out and confronting them now that their scheme had fallen apart. What amazed him was how simpleminded it seemed. He had thought they were weaving a more complicated plot than just trying the same swindle that had worked once before.

He slipped away, finding the narrow trail back down to the tailings where his horse was tethered. Belle and Corey ought to have learned not to go to the well too often or the dipper would eventually come up dry. When dealing with a man like George Hearst, you had to stay moving and agile, never repeating yourself.

Slocum started to leave the district but somehow he found himself heading back into Virginia City. He was missing something and not knowing what it was made him suspicious. It wouldn't hurt to talk with Hearst one more time. If nothing else, he could tell the mining magnate that he wasn't accepting his fine offer.

"Two hundred a week to do nothing," Slocum mused as he rode down C Street. All around saloons were brimming with thirsty miners and gamblers with keen eyes and no scruples. He shrugged it off. He was riding out of the Comstock district with far more money than he'd entered with. A man like him couldn't ask for any more.

He rode to Hearst's office and dismounted, only to find Hearst filling the doorway.

"Mr. Hearst, I wanted to—" Slocum was silenced by the man's volcanic explosion.

"You double-crossing sidewinder. I ought to throttle you

with my bare hands." Hearst took a step forward, his hands coming up as if to carry out his threat. Slocum stood his ground, wondering what the hell was going on.

"I'm turning down your offer," Slocum said before Hearst boiled over again. This time he had to step back or the huge man would have bowled him over. Hearst's face turned livid with rage.

"You stole it, you stole that mine!"

"What are you talking about?" Slocum wondered if Hearst had gone crazy. He wasn't making any sense.

"You're the worst thief I ever saw. I swear, Slocum, you'll get your comeuppance!" Hearst waved his hand, as if summoning someone.

Slocum didn't look behind him. He was more concerned with what Hearst might do. A man this size would pack quite a wallop if he took it into his head to swing.

"I don't know what you're talking about, Hearst," said Slocum. He widened his stance to draw, if he had to.

Then the world fell out from under him. Something hit him from behind and he pitched forward, striking his head against the boardwalk. He struggled to get to hands and knees and someone kicked him hard in the ribs.

"Take him into the alley, you fool," snapped Hearst. "Don't let anyone see you work him over. Then dump him outside of town. I don't want to see his ugly face in Virginia City again."

"Yes, sir," came the sarcastic reply. Through a red haze of pain, Slocum saw Hearst's shoes walk past. He tried to move and got another boot in the gut. He collapsed, fighting to suck in air.

"This is gonna be fun," he heard. He thought he recognized Luke Slade's voice, but he couldn't be sure. His eyes were clouding over. He felt strong hands grab him by the heels and drag him toward the alley running alongside Hearst's office.

Then he feebly struggled against a rain of fists that came from everywhere. Slocum curled up, taking several hard blows on the back. Protecting his belly gave him a chance to gasp in enough air to keep from passing out. Then he exploded like a coiled spring.

He flailed wildly and one hand struck his assailant, more by chance than design. Slocum still couldn't see clearly, but he kept swinging. He connected a second time and was rewarded with a dull grunt. He felt the man attacking him back off, possibly dazed. This gave him the only chance he was likely to get. He pulled his six-shooter and cocked it.

"Don't," he heard. Slocum moved slightly, aiming more by sound than sight. Tears filled his eyes. He wiped them free with his left hand even as his finger tightened on the hair-pull trigger on his Colt.

By the time Slocum's vision had cleared, the alley was empty. He thought it had been Luke Slade who'd blindsided him, but he couldn't be sure. Only Slade—or the man who had attacked him—and George Hearst would ever know for certain.

Slocum moaned and leaned back against the cold brick wall of Hearst's office building. He laid his six-gun across his lap and gingerly probed his ribs. He winced but didn't think anything was broken. His ribs were tender but only bruised. Standing, Slocum wobbled for a few steps, then found his strength flowing back. More than anything else, anger forced away any pain he might be enduring.

Slocum looked up and down the street, hunting for any sign of his attacker. The street was ominously empty, as if everyone knew Slocum was looking for someone to kill. This street lacking in any sign of life settled him a little. He staggered a few steps and found his stride by the time he reached the cross street leading to the land office.

Hearst had been furious, claiming he had been double-crossed. He had called Slocum a thief and a liar. The only place Slocum knew to get straight answers lay on the other side of the door he had jimmied once before.

Looking around and seeing only empty street, Slocum ducked down the alley and stood in front of the door. The wood hadn't been repaired; the land clerk might not have even known his office had been broken into twice before. Or he might not care. There wasn't anything of value to steal inside.

Slocum ran his fingers under the wood jamb and pried. Nails creaked and wood protested like some evil Indian death spirit, but it finally yielded and came free. The lock on the door was easily disengaged. Slocum slipped into the office and went straight for the ledger book standing open on the clerk's desk.

He ran his finger down the left page, squinting in the dim light coming through the front window. The past few days had been busy ones for the clerk. More than fifty claims had been filed.

But there was only one transfer of title. Slocum read it twice to be sure he wasn't imagining it.

Belladonna and Coreopsis Flowers had sold the Cuckoo Clock Mine yesterday for the sum of eight hundred thousand dollars.

To John Slocum.

15

Slocum's ribs throbbed as if somebody still drummed on them, but his head felt as if it were going to explode. The harder he tried to figure out just what the hell was going on, the worse the headache became. He sat on the floor of the land office and sucked in deep breaths, enduring the pain rippling through his chest.

"What have they done? Why?" Slocum shook his head and regretted it. This was as bad as the worst hangover he'd ever had. What was Belle doing to him?

When the torture in his chest died a mite, Slocum unsteadily got to his feet. His head still ached, and he wondered if he had hit it on the boardwalk harder than he'd thought. Anger boiled up and replaced the minor discomfort. He owed Slade for this, and he certainly owed George Hearst for not even doing his own dirty work. What did he owe Belle and Corey?

"Belladonna?" he said aloud, staring down at the ledger book. He had to laugh. Old Dalton Flowers had named his children well. Coreopsis was indeed a bright, sunny yellow flower always turning to follow the light. And Reed bent with the wind. The best of the lot, though, had to be Belle.

Belladonna. Nightshade. Pure poison.

Slocum left the office, shutting the door. He didn't care if anyone saw he had broken in. He had the churning feeling deep in his gut that he was in deep trouble. Walking slowly and stretching now and again until his strength came back and he worked some of the soreness from his muscles, he finally got to his gelding. The horse stared at him as if saying, "I told you so."

"We got a few more miles ahead of us," Slocum said, climbing into the saddle. "I got beat up and found out I'm supposed to be rich. We don't stop until I get even with everyone and have a cut of that eight hundred thousand."

The horse turned its head and looked back at him again before snorting wetly in disgust. Slocum interpreted this as meaning: "Humans can be so stupid."

He wasn't going to argue with his mount. The horse had better sense than he did sometimes. He knew the safest trail for him was one directly out of Virginia City, keeping the Washoe Zephyr at his back all the way. Getting Hearst mad at him was bad enough, but he thought the law would be coming after him before long. Whatever Belle and Corey had done, he was the one going to be left turning in the wind. If he didn't see a quick way out, he'd have to run.

But he hated the idea. Slocum wasn't the sort who turned tail when the going got tough. And he felt he was the one being swindled out of the money. There was no way in hell Belle could have found anyone willing to pay so much for the Cuckoo Clock so that meant it was all a ploy on her part. He just couldn't figure out what it was.

"She needs me to stick around town," Slocum said to his horse as he rode, thinking out loud. A wind like hot, fetid dying gasps blew into his face. Summer was beginning to burn the mountains and anyone foolish enough to be out under the sun.

"That's why she was willing to pay me so much—and offer me so much more than money." Slocum still couldn't decide why Hearst had offered him such a princely sum to stand around with his thumb stuck up his butt. That had to be part of some larger plan he didn't see, either.

He rode for almost an hour and got to the cutoff leading to the Cuckoo Clock Mine. Slocum paused and stared up the slope toward the mine, then straight ahead. He could make Reno in another day. In a week he could be in southern Oregon and away from all the trouble and confusion bubbling around him like some unsavory stew.

The gelding protested. It smelled freedom and safety blowing down from the north. Slocum did, too, but he had other irons in the fire. He had been warm and safe; mostly, he was wet, cold, and in a peck of trouble. Slocum didn't see any reason to change that now.

He neared the mine, then veered off the road. He doubted anyone would be here. Belle and Corey had made their pitch to Sam Hanrahan. Neither the Consolidated Virginia agent nor the Flowers sisters had much call coming back here now.

Still, Slocum remembered what had happened the first time Belle had sent him out to check "her" mines. He had killed Obadiah Clark for her and opened the way to a three-hundred-fifty-thousand-dollar sale. Slocum walked the last few hundred yards and waited almost ten minutes, just to be sure. He saw no one.

He saw no one but felt uneasy, as if someone was watching him from nearby.

He went into the small mining camp. The shack off to one side was unfit for any human or animal to live in. From its appearance, it might come tumbling down on anyone's head foolish enough to enter. A well outside it must have come up dry months and months ago. The wood bucket had dried in the sun and its staves had fallen off. Even the rope on the well's winch was turning brittle.

A few paces toward the mouth of the mine was the first of several small hills of abandoned equipment. The rusted machinery didn't seem to have much purpose; it had been dumped here for lack of any better place for it. Slocum examined the ground and saw nothing to alert him to anyone else's presence.

He looked around, though, wondering why he was so jumpy. That sixth sense of his was screaming and he saw no evidence for it. Slocum shrugged it off thinking that he wasn't back to normal yet after the beating Slade had given him.

Looking around outside the mine availed him nothing. He knew of the salted tailings; he'd heard Belle and Corey arguing over the price. But was the Cuckoo Clock worth anything? Reed Flowers had done a superficial job of salting it and had left proof where Hanrahan could see it. That didn't seem like anything Belle would tolerate—and Slocum had given the mine the once over earlier and had thought it was potentially a rich claim.

That meant she'd intended for Hanrahan to find the spent shotgun shell and to scrape off the thin silver patina blasted onto the walls. She wanted him to think this was the worthless hole in the ground that it was. That was the only conclusion Slocum could reach, but it didn't make much sense.

George Hearst and his partners in the Consolidated Virginia Company had the money to buy such a mine. Why go out of the way to make it look worthless when Belle and Corey wanted to sell it?

"Maybe it really *is* worth something," Slocum said, coming to the answer slowly. Even so, why not sell the mine to Hearst? Why go through the charade of selling it to him?

Slocum entered the mouth of the mine slowly, checking the timbers. Some had rotted away and others creaked under the ponderous weight of the mountain pressing on top of them. He went a few paces inside, found a carbide light, and managed to get it lit. Holding the light high, Slocum warily went deeper into the bowels of the mountainside.

Not fifty feet down the tunnel he found where Reed Flowers had shot the silver-laden shotgun shell into the walls. Slocum ran his fingers over the silver. It peeled off. Flowers hadn't done a good job, and this was what Hanrahan and his partner had seen. Slocum looked farther than the surface, though, needing to know if the Cuckoo Clock was worth the aggravation it was giving him.

Using the thick-bladed knife he carried sheathed at the small of his back, he scraped away at a view of quartz. It didn't appear promising. Fifteen minutes of digging showed him the rock didn't justify the backbreaking labor it would take getting it from the mine. Slocum explored a little farther, then smelled gas.

Hastily backing away, he turned and put down the carbide lamp. The water sloshing inside showed it was about empty. He turned off the light and hurried for the patch of light that was the mouth of the mine.

The gas bothered him, but not as much as the feeling of being crushed by the tons of rock above him. The timbers creaked ominously as the rock settled. Slocum stepped into the bright light of day—and almost died.

The first bullet sent his hat sailing. Not expecting to be ambushed, he followed his instincts and grabbed for his hat. It sailed away just beyond his reach, and this saved him from a second and third round that whizzed past. Slocum landed flat on his belly, the impact causing him to wince. His ribs might not have been broken, but they were tender as all get out.

He didn't have time to reflect on any of this. He scrambled for cover, more leaden death seeking him. Slocum rolled over onto his back, caught sight of the slope above the mine, and knew he was in big trouble. At least one bushwhacker with a rifle was up there.

He saw Slocum pass a rock overhang about the time Slocum saw him. Struggling to get his Colt Navy free, Slocum was slow getting a round off. The other man lifted his rifle and got off a good shot. Red-hot pain surged through Slocum's upper thigh as the bullet tore away a chunk of his flesh.

Slocum's second shot was better and drove the man to cover.

"We got 'im," came the shout from downslope. "Ain't no way he's gonna get away now!"

Slocum had to admit his future didn't look too bright. One man above him, at least two below, and he thought there might be three. A new round of bullets ricocheted off rocks just under his chin. He pulled back, wiping at the dust in his eyes. Slocum only had four rounds left, and he faced that many snipers.

That left him only one choice. He knew where the man upslope hid. The paltry pile of rocks wasn't much good protection, even if it was better than anything Slocum had. Slocum got to his feet, found the right way up, and charged.

He was exposed to fire from below, but his sudden move took the bushwhackers by surprise. They were just a fraction slow in responding, and one did what Slocum had hoped for. He shouted to his friend on the mountain.

"Hey, Big Nose, he's comin' your way!"

Big Nose rose up to see what was going on. Slocum fired three times. The third bullet found a home in the well-named man's face. Big Nose sagged limply and began sliding down the slope. Slocum fell flat and avoided a new fusillade of bullets, grabbing wildly for the dead man's rifle. He snared it just as a new hornet sting on his left arm sent a tiny fountain of blood spewing into the air.

"I got 'im. I got the son of a bitch!" cried the shooter. But he didn't have Slocum's sense when a shot was good and when it was just a tad off target.

Slocum lay still, waiting. His fingers curled around the rifle, tensing just enough so he wouldn't have to pull the trigger all the way back. He heard men start up after him from farther downslope. During the war Slocum had learned patience. Sometimes he would sit on a lonely hilltop all day, waiting, waiting, waiting. Then the time would come for him to act.

He spun over, rock cutting into his back. Slocum leveled the rifle and fired. The shot wasn't a killing one, but it took the lead man in the pit of the stomach and doubled him over. Slocum levered a new cartridge into the chamber and fired again. This one winged the second man. The third turned tail and ran for his life.

Slocum sat up and tried to get a clean shot at the fleeing man. There wasn't any way to do it. He turned back to the others. The one he'd gut-shot was in no condition to do much more than slowly bleed to death. Slocum slid down the hill and grabbed the man's rifle, then pulled his six-shooter from its holster.

The other man tried to get his six-gun up. Slocum had hit the man squarely in the shoulder, severely damaging the muscle. Wild panic flared when the man saw he didn't have the strength to use his right hand. Too late, he shifted his pistol to his left.

Slocum swung the butt of his rifle and caught the man under the chin, sending him rolling ass over teakettle until he fetched up hard against an overturned ore cart. The man moaned and kicked feebly. Slocum took his time going after him, making certain he had a round chambered in the captured rifle.

"Don't kill me, Slocum," the man pleaded.

Slocum's eyes narrowed as he studied the cringing man. He had never seen him before. He would have remembered if he had. Two pink scars formed a vivid X on the man's right cheek. And the one up the hill—Big Nose—had a look that wasn't easily forgettable, either. Slocum didn't bother with the man still sobbing in pain from the bullet in his belly. He knew he had never crossed paths with him.

"Who are you?" Slocum asked. "I don't know you. Why are you trying to kill me?"

The bullet sang through the air and glanced off the ore cart. The man stiffened, then rolled onto his side. Slocum ducked down, whipping the rifle barrel around. The man who had fled hadn't gone far. Another bullet ripped past Slocum's ear.

Dodging around the rusty cart, Slocum hunkered down and waited. The man he had been questioning had taken the slug just behind the ear, killing him instantly. Slocum wasn't sure if the bullet had been aimed to silence the man or had gone astray. It was likely the latter. Slocum was still the target, and the four men didn't look to just wounding him. From the start, they'd been out to gun him down.

Uphill the man Slocum had gut-shot stopped moaning. He'd either passed out or died. Slocum didn't know which and it didn't matter much to him. The man wasn't likely to rise up and shoot him in the back either way. Checking the captured weapons, Slocum saw he had four rounds left in the rifle and a full six shots in the pistol. The other rifle he'd dropped was halfway between him and the man on the hillside.

"Who are you?" Slocum called. "I think you got me confused with somebody else."

He knew it wasn't so. The man who'd been shot by his friend was proof the bushwhackers knew him. The dead man had called him by name.

"If I come out with my hands up, can we talk about this? I'm not the one you want."

"Go to hell, Slocum!" The four quick rounds that pinged off the ore cart told him his guess was right—they hadn't made any mistakes in finding their prey. And it also told him where the man was hiding. Not ten feet from the ramshackle tar-paper hut was a slight depression where water had run down from the mine.

The backshooter lay there, waiting for Slocum to make a mistake.

Slocum edged back behind the ore cart, knowing one of them had to make a move sooner or later. He was willing to outwait his opponent, but knowing where the man was gave him an advantage he was likely to lose if he waited too long. Slocum bent over farther, got his shoulders under the edge of the ancient cart, then heaved for all he was worth.

The heavy metal cart tipped onto its wheels but didn't roll. Slocum kept low as a new round of bullets whined past. He dug in his toes and pushed for all he was worth. The cart moved slowly, digging into the hard ground. Then Slocum found himself lying flat on his belly. The rusted wheels had broken free suddenly and the cart rattled down the hill directly for the water-eroded depression where the bushwhacker lay.

Slocum heard the cry of outrage and surprise, then got his chance. The man had to stand to get out of the way of the ore cart as it rumbled past him. If he had remained in the hollow, he would have been crushed by the cart.

Slocum got one shot. He squeezed it off and was rewarded with a yelp of pure agony. The man straightened up, threw his arms out, and fell backward. The sound of his body hitting the ground was music to Slocum's ears.

Scrambling forward, aware of the blood he was losing through the wound in his leg and the other in his arm, Slocum knew he had to finish this fast. He pulled out the six-shooter and cocked it.

The man lay flat on his back, his feet kicking feebly.

"You shot me in the spine. I feel all messed up inside. All liquid."

The bullet had caught the man a few inches above his waist, dead center in the middle of his back. Even if he lived, which Slocum wasn't sure was in the cards, he'd never walk again.

Slocum stared at the man, thinking hard what to do. There wasn't too much he could do. He'd left one, probably two, of the man's allies dead. And the man twitching feebly had plugged the third one, maybe trying to blow Slocum's head off. Slocum felt nothing for the man.

"How do you know me?" Slocum asked.

"Pocket. In my pocket." The man was fading fast. Slocum knew from the way the eyes were glazing over. They came unfocused and wandered around and only slowly came back to fix on him.

Slocum held the six-shooter carefully as he fished in the man's vest pocket with his left hand. He found a small slip of paper folded over. Pulling it out, Slocum flipped it open. His name was printed in block letters across the bottom. A crude sketch identified him better than most of the pictures on wanted posters floating around the West.

"Who gave this to you? Hearst?"

"No," the man croaked out. He licked dried lips. He swallowed hard and asked, "Water. Give me a drink of water."

"Who sent you to kill me?" Slocum repeated. He didn't want to ask, but he had to. "Was it Belle Flowers? Her sister?"

"No, don't know them."

"Reed Flowers?"

"Who?" The man coughed. "Water."

"Who paid you to kill me?" This was the question he should have asked to start, but Slocum had thought it would be faster if he found out George Hearst was behind the attempt.

"Mr. Parrish."

Slocum just stared at him. He didn't know any Parrish.

"Lawrence Parrish," the dying man said. He reached out for Slocum, his hand closing slowly. "Please. Water. I can't swallow. Mouth's like inside a cotton bale."

"Where do I find Lawrence Parrish?"

"Parrish Mill. Washoe."

Slocum backed off. The man kept begging for water. Slocum turned and went to his horse. There was no need wasting a single drop on that backshooter. Slocum mounted and headed his gelding toward Washoe to find Lawrence Parrish—and why he wanted him dead.

16

Slocum stopped on the rise and stared down into the dusty Washoe Valley. A mill and smelter at the far end looked like an obscene spider hanging in the middle of a monstrous web. Railroad tracks came from all over the valley, forming lacy lines feeding the voracious maw. Dust and greasy gray smoke were spewed forth in the process that tore precious metals from the raw ore. Where a dozen ore trains went into the mill, only one came out laden with gold and silver.

Slocum knew which it was by the look of the tracks and the small engine.

The ore trains were pulled by powerful engines and stretched forever with clanking cars mounded high with jagged rock. The locomotive leaving with the refined metal pulled only two freight cars, both heavily armored. Thoughts of what it would be like blocking the tracks outside the valley and sticking up that single train on its way to the secure banks of San Francisco ran through Slocum's mind—until he saw the troops of armed men waiting for the train to leave.

He squinted into the low afternoon sun and saw dozens of men enter the armored cars. He heaved a sigh. It would have been good getting away with hundreds of pounds of gold, but it wasn't in the cards. Too many other outlaws had tried and probably failed to pluck this ripe plum. Consolidated Virginia's owners couldn't afford to lose the end product of so much investment and sweat and death in their mines. Guarding the gold and silver shipments was probably the easiest part of the long chain running back far underground.

Swindling the company's owners out of their earnings seemed a better approach than using a six-shooter to rob them. And Slocum knew Belle and Corey had already taken it. He just had to figure out what was going on to get his cut of the very profitable pie.

"I sure as hell don't have eight hundred thousand hidden away," Slocum told his horse, "but I'd like to. And I will before I'm done with them all." The gelding snorted and shifted under him, as if calling him a fool for such high-falutin dreams.

Slocum turned and fumbled in his saddlebags until he found spare cylinders for his Colt Navy. He wanted enough firepower to be able to get out of any jam. He hadn't seen the four men who had almost bushwhacked him before going in. Slocum wasn't sure how that had happened because he had been alert.

"Not alert enough," he muttered, sliding two loaded cylinders into the pocket of his canvas duster. It wasn't enough to shoot his way free. Slocum recognized that as much luck as skill had kept him alive back at the mine shootout. He had to depend more on his own ability and less on luck.

Luck was too fickle to trust a second time.

Riding slowly, he went down into the Washoe Valley. It was like taking a dive in an ocean of smoke. The thick dust chocked him and made his eyes water. A narrow stream ran alongside the road, murky and brown and roiling with eye-burning chemicals. To drink from it would probably kill him; Slocum had to keep his horse's face turned from the stream. The horse wasn't any more immune from such poison than he was.

Twenty minutes later Slocum rode through the center of a small company town and went to the mill. He rubbed the dust from his eyes and peered through even thicker clouds to see the name painted with huge green letters on a rotted wood sign: Parrish Mill & Smelter.

The man hadn't been lying about there being a Parrish in Washoe—and Slocum didn't think the dying bushwhacker had been lying about Lawrence Parrish hiring him for the killing. All Slocum needed to know was why this Parrish felt so strongly about putting a new grave into the mountainside. Slocum had never met him and wasn't likely to get along like two pups in a basket with the mill owner anytime soon.

Slocum thought the mill and smelter must have been a good five miles distant, looking closer than it really was because of its immensity. Eight-story-tall smokestacks spewed out their smoke, and heavy brick buildings filled with clanking machinery dwarfed a man standing beside them. Pipes thicker than his body poured out their brown sludge into the river he had seen earlier; upstream the water was clear enough for drinking. Below the mill it turned into pure corruption on an immense scale. It was as if everything in the smelter had been built with some giant operator in mind, and any man who blundered in was nothing more than a bug to be crushed.

It made Slocum feel small just looking at the mill.

Riding around the building told Slocum nothing. He had to wipe the dirt from his face continually to the point that he pulled his bandanna up, as if he'd been caught in a West Texas dust storm. The mill was noisy and dirty and incredibly profitable, if Slocum was any judge.

Even as he rode around, he saw a small train leaving. Armed guards sat on the roof of the two mail cars, their eyes constantly roving. Several saw Slocum and turned their shotguns in his direction. Slocum kept his horse from dancing too close to the railroad tracks. He watched the train vanish, wondering if they were likely to report his presence. Around so much wealth, men got jumpy.

And with good reason.

Slocum's horse reared and almost unseated him when a steam whistle sounded. Slocum got control again and calmed the gelding. He pulled out his brother Robert's watch and peered at the dial. A little past six. The whistle must have signaled the end of a shift. Slocum saw a thin stream of men filing from the mill as others went in.

A slow smile crossed his lips. He wasn't getting anywhere riding around, wondering what to do next. A drink would do him a world of good, a few dollars spread around a saloon might loosen tongues to give him some idea what he was up against. He turned his horse toward the line of workers plodding into their town. It didn't take him long to see where most of them were headed.

Slocum entered the Crushed Ore Saloon behind the last of the dirty, tired mill workers. He blinked in surprise at what he found. The inside of the saloon was as dirty as the air outside. Everywhere he looked was a thick covering of fine dust from the mill. Nobody took cleaning very seriously. Even in the best of saloons Slocum expected to find traces of last week's clientele, but this saloon was filthy.

It took a few seconds for him to realize he had trouble telling the difference between the mill workers and the bar they leaned against. Everything was a uniform brown.

"What kin I gitcha?" the barkeep asked.

"Whiskey," Slocum said, knowing he'd get trade whiskey laced with gunpowder and rusty nails for body. He stared at what the barkeep poured for him and hesitated to even touch it.

"Where'd this come from, the river?" he asked. The liquor had the same color as the river running turgid with tailings from the mill. Slocum sloshed it around and saw that it discolored the sides of the shot glass. He had often heard cowboys order a "shot of poison" when they came into a bar. This was the first time he'd ever seen it served up without any comment.

"You want it or not?" the barkeep demanded.

"I'll take it, mister," the stocky mill worker next to him said. The way the man's hands shook told the story. Slocum silently pushed it over.

"That'll be two dollars," the barkeep demanded truculently. "I ain't runnin' no charity."

"You ain't runnin' nothing no how, Burke," the mill worker said. "This here gin mill's owned by Parrish, just like everything else in this damned town." He sampled the whiskey and then drank it down, as if it were good. "Hell, Parrish owns the town and everyone in it. Me included."

"Another?" asked Slocum. He motioned and the barkeep glowered but filled the glass again.

"Sure am obliged. They was talkin' about cuttin' me off here."

"You're a damned deadbeat, that's what you are, O'Leary."

"Yeah, sure, a deadbeat you calls me." O'Leary turned to Slocum and stared him in the eye. "You got the look of prosperity. You wouldn't know what it's like in a company town."

"Tell me," Slocum said. He pushed two twenty-dollar greenbacks across and took the bottle from the bartender. He guided O'Leary to a table near the door.

"That I will, that I will," O'Leary said, his voice husky from the booze. He knocked back another drink and wiped his lips. Dirt smeared and gave him a hideous aspect. Slocum thought of Indians and war paint, but they painted to look brave, not cadaverous. Dirt filled the hollows of O'Leary's cheeks and dark circles under his eyes made him look like a raccoon.

"I know a thing or two about company towns," Slocum said.

"Then you know what a jackass men like Burke are." O'Leary jerked his thumb back in the barkeep's direction. "He works direct for Parrish, he does. He don't have to break his back sixteen hours a day just to stay even."

"From the sound of it, you're not even staying even." Slocum knew how company towns worked. The only place to buy food and other necessities from was a company-owned store—and the prices charged were ten times fair market. The bills owed were subtracted from a worker's salary, often leaving him farther in the hole at the end of a month than when he started. He might work impossible hours for piss-poor shelter and food provided by the company, and still be in debt.

"Sixteen damned hours a day, six days a week. And I'm thinking about a shift on Sundays. You'd think, you would, that I'd ne'er have time to spend the money." O'Leary shook his greasy-haired head. "Don't work like that. There's always somethin' more they take from me. If I didn't have a wife and wee ones at home, I'd take off and find decent work, I would."

"The whiskey helps the pain," Slocum said.

"You *do* understand, and here I was thinkin' you were a company man. You got the look of them scabs Parrish brings in now and again whenever we try to organize." O'Leary stretched, his joints cracking like thunder. "Often times, I can't even bend my fingers. When I do, the pain's more'n any decent man can stand." O'Leary abandoned any pretense of drinking from the glass and worked straight on the bottle. Slocum said nothing as the man drank.

"You're a saint. You don't work for the company. Ain't no way," O'Leary rattled on.

"I am looking for some men who work for the company." Slocum described the four men who had tried to murder him the best he could. "One's known as Big Nose. And another's got an X-marked scar on his right cheek." Slocum moved his finger to show where. He saw O'Leary turn pale under the thick layer of dirt on his face.

"I know them," the mill worker said. "You want to steer clear of them, I tell you true. Them four is bad news for anyone crossin' 'em."

"I have some business with them." Slocum said, not bothering to tell O'Leary he'd already killed the men.

O'Leary bent forward. In a breath strong enough to fell a buffalo, he said, "They're Parrish's bully boys. Killed more workers than there're stars in the sky."

"Can't see many through the dust," Slocum observed.

"They're killers. You got the look, too, which is why I thought you was one of 'em. But you sound like you got business with them." The way O'Leary said *"business"* it was certain he knew Slocum and the four killers weren't friends.

"They work for Lawrence Parrish?" Slocum motioned to the barkeep for another bottle. O'Leary was almost falling from his chair in a dead drunk, but he needed more information.

"They kill for the son of a bitch." O'Leary started snickering, then burst out laughing. He got to laughing so hard, he had to hold his belly with both arms.

"What's so funny?" Slocum asked when the first gales of laughter abated.

"Just thinkin' about Parrish and Hearst. Heard tell they got skunked good and proper. That's enough to keep all Parrish's bully boys busy for a month of Sundays."

"How's this?" Slocum tensed. He had the feeling of being near the payoff for buying forty dollars' worth of rotgut whiskey.

"Parrish and Hearst—both of 'em are partners in Consolidated Virginia—got rooked out of a valuable mine. Everyone's talkin' about it."

"Who did it?"

"Some slicker from the Dakotas, heard tell," O'Leary said. "He snuck in a bid on the biggest mine in the whole damn Comstock Lode since Old Pancake did the Grosch boys out of their claim over in Gold Canyon. Heard he romanced the women what owned the mine so they sold cheap. Parrish was fit to be tied, and I reckon Hearst ain't in better condition."

"So this gent from South Dakota romanced the owners and got it on the sly?"

"Got damn near everything on the sly. They sold to him for a fraction of the value. Millions to be had in the mine, they say. Millions!"

O'Leary fell to the floor, laughing hard. Slocum stared at him and knew he wasn't likely to get any more information from the drunk mill worker.

Slocum knew who the rumors were about—him. It was becoming clear to him what was going on. Reed Flowers was probably the one spreading the rumors about the romancing. It wouldn't be seemly for either Belle or Corey to do that. But they certainly had a great deal to do with stories of the Denver slicker and the value of the Cuckoo Clock Mine.

Slocum shook his head in wonder. They had done a fine job setting him up for the likes of Hearst and Parrish to come after him for hornswoggling them out of a valuable mine, but men like them didn't operate on rumor. Something had convinced them the Cuckoo Clock was worth far more than the eight hundred thousand Slocum supposedly paid. After Hanrahan and the other Consolidated Virginia agents had reported the mine had been salted and was worthless, what evidence would it take for Hearst—and Parrish—to think otherwise?

An idea came to Slocum. He stepped over O'Leary on the way out of the saloon. He stared up at the mine, sending huge plumes of smoke and dust into the air, and knew where he could find out what he needed to know.

A single oil lamp burned in the offices of the Parrish Mill and Smelter Company office. Other nearby offices carried names of no interest to Slocum, but one caught his eye painted in gilt on a window halfway down the dingy street. Consolidated Virginia had a large office here. It made sense that the company controlled most every aspect of gold and silver production in the Comstock Lode. They made profit on mining, on smelting, on selling supplies to those doing the work—and then they reaped immense profits from the metal itself.

Slocum rode past Parrish's office, glancing inside. A man sat hunched over a table, working furiously on a huge ledger. It had been a long, hard day and Slocum wasn't inclined to pussyfoot around, but he had seen more than just the man working on the ledger.

Next to the man's right hand on the table lay a cocked six-shooter. He wouldn't much cotton to Slocum or anyone else barging in on him.

Slocum considered what the gun meant. There might be money in the office safe, or the company town might just be dangerous for a man so far up in Parrish's company. Whatever the cause, Slocum wasn't going to tangle with the accountant. He kept his horse walking until he came to the end of the block, then reined back and dismounted. It was time to see if he had learned anything all the years he'd been out West.

Slocum found an alley and stopped for a moment to stare at the door. He had an uneasy sense that he'd done this before, that he was breaking into the land office back in Virginia City. Reaching out, he turned the knob slowly. Unlike the land office door, this one wasn't locked. He entered quietly, using every trick of stealth he had ever learned.

The accountant never looked up from his work. The oil lamp flickered a little and the man turned up the wick so he got a purer light. Other than this, he never turned from his work.

Slocum knew it would be easier to walk over and slug the man. Hell, as mean as he was feeling, shooting the son of a bitch in the back wasn't too farfetched a thing to do. He worked for Parrish, and Parrish had sent four killers out on a bushwhacking job. Slocum touched his Colt, then relaxed. The man might work for Parrish, but that didn't mean he shared in Parrish's wealth.

From the tattered cuffs and the way he hurried to finish, Slocum thought the accountant was as trapped as a fly in amber—or O'Leary and all the other workers in the mill.

Slocum duckwalked across the room, moving slowly, not making a sound. He came to a bookcase filled with ledgers similar to the one the accountant pored over. Slocum worked his way down the rows until he found one not quite returned to the shelf. He had to restrain himself from crowing in triumph. This was what he needed to see.

The ledger contained records of recent ore shipments sent to the Parrish Mill for smelting. Along with the source would be the assay report and some evidence of how much silver had been produced.

Slocum pulled the book from the shelf and it fell open to a page smudged with dozens of fingerprints, as if many people had been studying what was recorded here.

He saw his name written in block letters as being the owner of the Cuckoo Clock Mine. Preliminary shipments a day earlier from the mine for smelting had been sent. The date, transportation information, and details Slocum wasn't interested in were meticulously recorded.

Then he found the line he needed. Again he had to restrain himself from letting out a low whistle. The ore sent from the Cuckoo Clock smelted out to four thousand dollars per ton, the richest strike in the district since MacKay, Fair, Hearst, and the others had formed the Consolidated Virginia Company by taking over the Hale-Norcross and the Ophir.

Slocum didn't have to return to the Cuckoo Clock to know that what he'd taken for salted tailings had been sent to Parrish for smelting. Belle was using the mounds of ore she'd bought elsewhere and shipped in to dupe Hanrahan. She'd saved it to sucker Parrish into believing he, Hearst, and the others had been swindled out of the mine.

And the swindler was a slicker from South Dakota named John Slocum.

17

Slocum slid the ledger back onto the shelf carefully, then tried to make his way out of the smelter office. He never knew what it was that alerted the accountant. Maybe Slocum tried to move too fast and carelessly dragged a boot sole on the wood floor. Maybe the accountant just happened to turn around to fetch another book. Whatever it was, things moved fast.

The accountant let out a yelp of surprise and went for the six-shooter beside his hand. Slocum was bent over and unable to go for his own Colt. The first shot belonged to the man at the table, and it was almost enough to do Slocum in. The slug ripped through his duster and a hot lance of fire exploded in his belly. Slocum let out a cry of pain and tumbled backward.

"You thievin' son of a bitch!" the accountant roared. He worked hard at getting the six-gun cocked for a second shot.

Slocum lay stunned on the floor, wondering why he wasn't dead. His duster had flopped open. Looking down at his belly, he saw the reason. The bullet had glanced off his belt buckle. Pieces of lead and silver had blasted into

Slocum's stomach, but he wasn't gut-shot, and he was a long way from being dead.

He jerked to one side, then whirled to go in the other as a second report filled the office. The accountant started cursing a blue streak about robbers. Slocum wondered if there was enough money in the office to make it worth his while to kill the man and then rob Parrish.

He fetched up hard against a desk just as the third shot blew splinters off the floor less than an inch from his face. Slocum quit worrying about robbery and started thinking on staying alive. His hand slipped over the butt of his six-shooter. He drew and fired in a practiced move that ripped a shriek of fear from the accountant's throat. The man blundered back into his table, upsetting the oil lamp.

In seconds the room turned into an inferno.

Slocum didn't think he'd struck the accountant, but it hardly mattered. The man's oil-soaked clothing had turned him into a torch. He burst through the front door and into the street, waving his arms wildly as he burned. The accountant drew attention to himself and the blaze in the office. Slocum fought his way through the fire and got to the back door.

Two men stood there, fear on their faces.

Slocum yelled, "He's trapped inside. Couldn't get him. Rescue him." He pointed into the heart of the fire. Even if someone had still been inside, there was no way short of a miracle any rescue could be made. Slocum pushed between the men and stumbled into the street. He saw the accountant lying in the middle of the street. He had stopped screaming. He had stopped living.

Slocum felt nothing for the man except a strange hollow feeling. He hadn't known him and bore him no malice. He had been nothing more than some poor fool trying to keep alive working for slave's wages. But he had brought on his own death. If he hadn't started shooting, Slocum would have been long gone with no one the wiser.

Fire bells began ringing up and down Washoe Valley. In a few minutes, hundreds of men would be forming bucket brigades in an attempt to save the town. Slocum had smelled the burnt wood when he'd first ridden into Virginia City. The Corporation Tower, a tall stone spire set up above the expensive houses on Gold Hill, provided that town a fire lookout. As he mounted and turned his gelding away from the dancing flames, he wondered if Parrish would build a similar structure to warn of future fires in his smaller town.

He doubted it. He doubted Parrish would even let the men working the midnight shift at the mill help put out the fire. The Consolidated Virginia Company might lose a few minutes work on the ore piled two stories high outside the mill.

Slocum reached the rim of the Washoe Valley and stopped at the spot where he had first seen the mill earlier in the day. The bright tongues of flame licking upward through the smoke looked like a vision of hell. He sat for several minutes watching the company town go up in thick clouds of smoke, then turned and rode back for Virginia City. He had business there.

As he covered the fifteen miles between the mill and Virginia City, Slocum thought hard. He was still alive. Maybe this ought to be enough for him. He had more money riding in his shirt pocket, even after all the wild spending he'd done, to keep him happy for a year or longer. He should turn his horse's face for the north and ride like all the demons of hell were nipping at his heels.

He ought to do that, but he didn't. He'd been ambushed and shot up and made the dupe in some scheme he didn't understand yet. How could Belle and Corey Flowers make a dime out of Hearst by pretending that Slocum had bought the Cuckoo Clock Mine? The evidence was clear.

It looked as if Slocum had somehow duped Sam Hanrahan into reporting that the mine was worthless, that it had been salted in a slapdash way any novice miner could see. Hanrahan had told George Hearst the mine was worthless and then Slocum came riding in, the apparent new owner. It was impossible for the rich ore to be sent to Parrish's mill without word getting back to Hearst.

Hanrahan was probably out of a job because he had missed the real value in the Cuckoo Clock. And Slocum was everyone's target because he'd supposedly ridden in from the Dakotas with wads of money to buy the richest mine opened since the Ophir.

Slocum laughed harshly. Hanrahan had done his job well, steering Hearst away from the deal. And Slocum had done nothing more than dress up in fancy duds, play poker one night, and let himself be shown around as a mining engineer. He was the fall guy, but he still had some of the money Belle had paid him.

And memories. He had memories of both sisters that were priceless.

"If they were in my sights right now," he told his horse, "would I pull the trigger? On Corey? On Belle?" Slocum didn't have a good answer for that. But he did owe Luke Slade for a beating, and anything he could do to Hearst and Parrish was due them.

He had a powerful lot of scores to settle.

When he got to Virginia City, it was close to four in the morning. From the crowd in the Howling Wilderness, though, it might have been eight at night. The drunken cheers from inside told him the miners were tying on one in celebration of someone hitting it big. There wasn't any other reason for the saloon to be so crowded this far into the night. Most of the saloon patrons ran out of money by midnight or got too stinking drunk to do more than get robbed by the whores. Either way it usually quieted down.

He dismounted and tethered his horse at a drinking trough. He owed the gelding more than its fill of water, but it was too late to put the horse into the stable. If he waited an hour, the ostler would be up and working on the horses in his charge.

That gave Slocum time to get some of the dust and smoke out of his mouth.

The Howling Wilderness was packed so tight with drunk miners he had to shoulder his way through to get to the bar. A bottle was making the rounds, each miner taking a swig and passing it along. Slocum got a good swallow and let out a sigh of contentment. This wasn't as good as the liquor over at the Cassandra Club, but it was a sight better than he'd been given at the Washoe Valley saloon.

And he never wanted to think again about the poison he'd been served at Parrish's company saloon.

"What's the celebration for?" he shouted to the man next to him. The grizzled old miner didn't even look in his direction as he answered.

"There's been a new strike. Rich! We're all gonna be rich. Most mines have been playin' out for years. Not even the Ophir's the mine it was even a year back. But the Cuckoo Clock's gonna make us all rich when that son of a bitch is dead."

"Who's that?"

"Some yahoo name of Slocum. George Hearst's promised us all jobs when Slocum's strung up and he's the new owner."

Slocum went cold inside. "If the mine's so rich, why lynch the owner?"

"He's bringin' in his own crew from the Dakotas, the slimy bastard. We done made Virginia City what it is. How dare he let us starve? I say, good for George Hearst and the Consolidated Virginia Company!"

The miner's words fell across the room as a momentary lull settled in. As the sentiment sunk in, there came a rousing cheer for the man Slocum would as soon kill as talk to. He pulled his hat lower on his face and wished he hadn't spent so much time in the Howling Wilderness. Any number of these men might be able to identify him.

He almost made it into the street. He pushed open the door and started to duck out, only to run smack into Luke

Slade. The gunman bristled that anyone would have the nerve to bump into him, then a look of astonishment spread on his face when he recognized Slocum.

"You!" the gunman bellowed. His hand was moving for his six-shooter even as he spoke.

Slocum was in no position to draw. Slade had stepped back. Slocum took two quick strides and swung as hard as he could, not going for his pistol. He hit Slade square in the gut. The man folded like a bad poker hand and dropped to his knees. His fingers twitched feebly, straining to tighten on his gun butt. Slocum didn't give him the chance to recover. He stepped back, then launched a kick that ended on the tip of Slade's chin. The gunman dropped to the boardwalk outside the saloon, out cold.

The fight had taken only seconds, but miners inside the saloon had been drawn like flies to fresh horse shit.

"Go on, give it to 'im!" encouraged one miner. "Never did like Slade all that much."

Cheers went up, then died when someone shouted, "That's him. That's John Slocum! The one what Hearst wants!"

Slocum didn't stand around to argue. He vaulted over Slade's body and hit the street, only to pull up short. As if a telegraph wire had been strung between all the saloons, men poured into the street from several others in front of him. Slocum spun, looking to backtrack.

The Howling Wilderness was empty now, all the miners wanting a piece of his hide. He didn't know how much Hearst was offering, but it must be one whale of a lot. Slocum knew better than to pull his pistol and start firing. Dozens of men were after him. If he killed one or two, he would be lucky—and the crowd would be even madder. They might rip him limb from limb rather than waiting for someone to get a knotted rope to string him up.

Slocum feinted right and dodged to the left, finding a dark alley. The roar going up behind him gave him some idea how a fox felt when the pack of hounds was loosed. He had to find a secure burrow to hole up in. But where?

He didn't look behind him. He heard the thunder of heavy boots in the dirt. Boardwalks rattled and men cursed while others cheered them on. He wasn't going to get away unless he did something quick. Slocum got into A Street, skidded around, took a quick reconnoiter, and dived into the side door of a sleepy little saloon. Only a half-dozen men drank here, mostly ready to call it a night. No one even looked up when he sank into a chair by a window where he could peer through the dirty windowpane into the street.

Two men did turn to stare through the swinging doors opening on the street when the crowd surged past. A man from the mob stuck his head inside and declared, "We got him! We got the son of a bitch!"

"Who's that?" asked the barkeep.

"The one Hearst's posted the five-hundred-dollar reward for."

Slocum swallowed hard. Men with limitless finances could afford such huge rewards. He had been dogged with the charge of killing a carpetbagger judge ever since he'd left the family farm in Calhoun, Georgia, and most of the rewards offered for him never amounted to more than a hundred dollars. Slocum had considered this a princely enough sum until he'd come to Virginia City.

Here the gold and silver made millionaires out of a few and men willing to do anything to become millionaires out of the rest.

"Let's go get 'im!" cried a drunk at the bar. He turned and ran into another man. The pair tumbled to the floor. The bartender laughed, then vaulted the wide oak bar and landed heavily. He carried a short club that swung from a wrist strap as if it were loaded with lead shot.

"You two watch the store," the barkeep said to one man staying behind. "I can use the reward." The man charged out. Slocum slumped over the stained table, trying to will himself into as small a profile as possible. He couldn't fight the entire town.

He ought to hightail it out of Virginia City, but he couldn't. He wouldn't. He had been used, beat up, lied to, shot, and now hung out to cure like some prize ham. He wasn't sure what got his bristles up the most. Hearst putting out a reward for him was bad enough.

Even if everything Hearst thought about him was true, Slocum hadn't done anything to set the town on his heels like a pack of mad dogs. He hated lynch mobs, and that was what Hearst had unleashed. But being used by Belle rankled the most.

Slocum turned his head to one side and scanned the saloon. The men the barkeep had left to run things were behind the bar and helping themselves to the whiskey. He didn't worry about them. Two others were out cold, spilled whiskey around them. But the remaining patron sat and just stared at Slocum, as if trying to remember where he had seen him before.

Slocum stood and headed for the back door, knowing it wouldn't be long until the man remembered. He reached the door leading into the storeroom when the man called out, "I know you. You're the mangy cayuse what wants to put us all out of work!"

A flash of light off a gun's barrel alerted Slocum. He dropped to the floor, drew, and fired before his attacker could get off his shot. His slug caught the man high on the head. Flopping around, the man hit the ground and kicked wildly, screaming as he struggled. Blood flowed everywhere but Slocum didn't think he had seriously injured the man. Head wounds bled like a stuck pig and weren't often that serious.

The single report had echoed down the streets like a clarion call to the crowd hunting Slocum. They came running. Slocum kicked in the storeroom door and tumbled inside. He slammed it behind him and found a large barrel of whiskey to roll against the door. Slocum sat on the barrel for a moment to catch his breath. Then he looked around to see how to get out.

"Damnation," he muttered. He had trapped himself. There was only one window, and it was high up and too small for him to ever wiggle through. From the sound out in the saloon, it wouldn't take the man he'd winged more than a few seconds to point where he'd taken refuge.

Almost as if thinking it brought his worst fears to life, the storeroom door creaked as someone threw his shoulder against it. The door creaked again and nails began to pop out of the wood. Slocum heard men shouting at each other, trying to get a battering ram to finish off the door—and Slocum.

The ceiling didn't offer any escape; it was too high and looked secure. But the floor was different. Every step Slocum took made it sag and creak. Trying to ignore the way the door hinges were giving way and the triumphant shouts of the men waiting to turn him over to Hearst for their reward, Slocum began prying up the floorboards. He ripped away one board, then another. He didn't have time for a third.

The storeroom door exploded inward, bringing three men with it. Others scrambled over their backs, waving pistols and shouting orders at each other. But Slocum had seen his only chance and took it. He forced himself between the floorboards and landed in muck under the saloon.

Only the sudden entry by so many men saved him. Someone kicked a loose floorboard back into place, and the pushing and shoving caused the eager mob to ignore the other loose planks.

"What is he, some kind of ghost? Where the hell'd he go?" demanded someone.

"Maybe Jennings was wrong. That shot to the head might have scrambled his brains."

"What brains?" countered another. "He ain't been right since that mule kicked him a year ago this summer."

Slocum lay on his back, staring up through broad cracks at the boot soles of the men hunting him. The crowd milled around in the storeroom until someone mentioned the whiskey barrel and its contents. The men roared in approval and rolled it into the saloon's main parlor. Slocum heaved a sigh of relief. In a few minutes the whiskey would be passed out—and in a few more the men would be passed out, too.

Wiggling like a worm, he made his way through the mud until he came to the saloon's outer wall. He tried to pry free a board and escape into the night, but he couldn't get one loose. He worked his way up and down the wall, almost crushed by the sagging floor above him. With less than a foot of crawlspace, he couldn't get enough leverage to force open an escape path.

Tired, frustrated, and beginning to feel the effect of being trapped under the saloon, Slocum held back a rising tide of panic.

"Think it through," he whispered to himself. The sound of his own voice calmed him a mite, but he was still in big trouble and that spooked him. "Back out the way you came," he decided. Slithering like a snake, Slocum returned to the storeroom floor and pushed up a loose board. The room was empty but he saw the revelers in the saloon beyond. The barrel of whiskey was still half full, and this attracted more of the lynch mob from the streets.

Slocum saw hints that daylight wasn't far off. He couldn't stay where he was much longer or he'd succumb to the panic gnawing away at him. He had worked in mines and didn't notice the closed-in feeling over much. But now he was sure the saloon floor would cave in on him and crush him flat. Staying was the safest thing he could do.

He had to leave.

The relief he felt as he left the crawlspace behind was almost more than he could take. Slocum sucked in deep breaths and tried to still his racing heart. He had faced men he knew were faster, who were better shots, and he had come out a winner. But his own fears almost did him in now.

"Whatcha gonna do with the reward money when we catch him?" a drunken miner just on the other side of the wall asked an unseen companion.

"Get the hell out of here. Been a year or more since I saw the wife and kids."

"Me, I don't have no wife. Maybe I got kids, but no woman's ever tole me about 'em."

The two continued talking. Slocum stood and slipped to the door and judged his chances for escaping. Most of the miners in the saloon were intent on the whiskey. The man he'd shot in the head sat at a table and told and retold the story of Slocum's fabulous shot and how he had faced him down and was owed a cut of the reward when Slocum was caught.

Slocum knew he had to act. He settled himself, then walked out boldly. He dripped mud from under the saloon but few of the miners were in better condition. If anything, the dirt kept them from recognizing him.

Slocum got to the side door and reached for the knob when a cold voice behind said, "Take another step and I'll blow your damn head off!"

He froze, waiting for the bullet that would take his life.

18

"Where do you think you're going?" came the cold question.

"Out," Slocum said, wondering if he could draw and fire without getting cut down. He didn't have a snowball's chance in hell if the man had the drop on him. "Got to take a leak."

"You ain't paid for the whiskey you drank."

"Thought it was free," Slocum said, relaxing a mite. The man hadn't identified him—he just thought he saw a deadbeat leaving without paying. "Nobody else is coughing up any money for it."

"The barkeep put me in charge," the man behind Slocum said. "Gimme five dollars and you can go."

Slocum knew extortion when he heard it. He also knew he had to get out of the saloon without the others noticing him. Five dollars was a small price to pay.

"Here it is," he said, fumbling in his shirt pocket. The thick wad of money there was dwindling and had taken quite a beating. It was soaked through with sweat and muck, but Slocum still had a passel more than he'd had when he rode into Virginia City. All he had to do now was get out of town alive if he wanted to spend it.

"What's wrong? Get your ass back here and give it to me."

Slocum turned, hoping the mud on his face would conceal his identity. He held the ten-dollar bill out where the other man could see it.

"This is all I got. Give me some change and it's yours."

The man's eyes danced from the bill to Slocum's face and back. For a moment Slocum thought he was going to escape for the price of a ten-dollar greenback. Then the man's eyes darted back and hardened with recognition. Slocum acted. He took two quick steps forward and said loudly, "Here's your damned money."

He jammed the bill into the man's face with his left hand even as his right swung in a short arc that ended in the man's belly. As the man started to fall, Slocum caught him.

"What's wrong? Can't hold your liquor?" He laughed harshly and put his chin down on his chest to keep others nearby from seeing him clearly. He need not have bothered. They were too busy working on the dregs in the whiskey barrel. How so few men had drunk so much of the potent liquor was beyond Slocum, but he was grateful. They had to be staggering drunk and unable to focus on anything beyond their shot glasses.

Slocum got his arm under the man's arms and pulled him toward the door. Slocum took one last glance around the saloon and didn't see anyone paying him any mind. Grunting, he lugged the man into the alley running alongside the saloon, then dropped him to the ground. Slocum stuffed the ten back into his pocket, then dropped down beside the man, who stirred feebly, retching from the blow to his belly.

"You just sleep it off," Slocum said loudly, noticing sudden interest from the street. A half-dozen men carrying ax handles or shotguns had stopped to see what was going on. "That rotgut surely does pack a wallop."

Someone in the small lynch mob made a crude comment and the others laughed. Then they drifted away, still hunting for their elusive quarry. Slocum turned back to the man struggling to get his breath back and swung again, this time landing the barrel of his pistol along the man's temple. A sick crunch put the man out colder than a cod.

Slocum stood and watched the fallen man for a few seconds before deciding he wasn't going to cause any more trouble. Cutting his throat would prevent a hue and cry being raised when the man came to, but Slocum didn't have the stomach for it. The man might have been willing to turn him over to a lynch mob for a few dollars, but Slocum had no feud with him. Killing him might not gain him any time, either.

Slocum had people to find and little time to do it. The false dawn lighting the sky with bright grays and dull pinks promised a bright, sunny Nevada day in less than an hour. He had to finish his business by then or he'd be a sitting duck for anyone with a six-shooter.

He found his horse and mounted, deciding revenge could wait. He wanted to find Belle and Corey and get to the bottom of their swindle. Time wore heavily on him so he put his heels into the gelding's flanks, urging the horse up Union Street at a pace certain to draw attention. People looked at him but no one reacted with a flying bullet or shotgun blast. The mud he'd wallowed in under the saloon hid his face enough to give him a head start.

Slocum slowed when he saw a tight knot of men making their way down Gold Hill, going from house to house. He rode straight up the steep slope until he got to a street running parallel and behind the fashionable houses. Slocum reined back and just waited, partially hidden by a small stand of trees. The lynch mob met with the kind of reception he'd expected. Knocking on the doors of rich people just before sunrise wasn't too smart.

Angry shouts were the least responses. A few shots were fired at the mob, dispersing them. Someone decided Slocum must be hiding farther down the hill in Virginia City, and the others quickly took up this sensible notion. In five minutes the would-be posse had vanished and the people in the lavish houses on Gold Hill began to stir for their normal morning schedules.

Slocum dismounted and walked his horse toward Belle's house, approaching from the rear. He saw deep cuts in the dirt showing where a heavily laden carriage had traveled recently. A closer examination showed a horse pacing the carriage. Slocum considered taking out after what had to be Belle and Corey, then decided a quick search of their house might be more profitable. It wouldn't take long and could give him valuable information.

In the back of his mind, Slocum thought he might even find some of the money from their swindle. Enough fresh greenbacks riding in his saddlebags could make him forgive and forget a great deal.

"Stay here for a while longer," Slocum told his horse. The gelding edged toward a feed trough, still filled with oats. Slocum let the animal eat. It might have to carry him out of the Comstock district at top speed later.

He went up the rear steps to the porch leading from the kitchen. He peered inside and saw no one. He went to the kitchen door and gingerly turned the knob. To his surprise the door was open. Slocum ducked in, aware that more people stirred. Anything suspicious might bring down the wrath of a lynch mob on him, if a neighbor happened to mention it to the wrong people. He drifted through the kitchen into the parlor where Belle and Corey had spent so much of their time.

Slocum paused, wondering what felt wrong about the house. Then it hit him. The furniture was covered with sheets, as if they intended to be gone for some time. He made a hasty search of the downstairs, finding nothing. Slocum hurried upstairs. The bedrooms were similarly shrouded. He went into Belle's room and pulled the muslin sheet from a dresser. A few pieces of cheap jewelry remained, but what caught his attention was a small box tied with red grosgrain ribbon.

He seized the small box and untied the ribbon. Inside were dozens of letters. Slocum settled down on the edge of the bed and pawed through the correspondence for some clue as to where Belle might have gone. The more of the letters he read, the more confused he became.

Not a one of the letters was addressed to—or from—Belle Flowers. The names were almost familiar. Slocum thought hard, then remembered. The names mentioned in the letters were those of the Hamilton family, a San Francisco family with banking and mining interests. He looked around the rest of the rooms and confirmed what he had guessed. Belle and Corey had simply moved into the Hamilton house, using it for their own ends while the real owners were absent.

He dropped the letters back into the box and put it in its place on the dresser, then tossed the sheet over the furniture. Slocum hurried down the stairs. He had to catch Belle before her carriage stopped leaving tracks he could follow. This house was a dead end, as so much else was about her.

Slocum stepped out onto the kitchen porch and froze. Something wasn't right.

"We got you in our sights, Slocum. Give up." Slade's cold voice carried just a hint of gloating. "Hearst's put up a five-hundred-dollar reward for you. That'll look mighty fine riding in my pocket."

Slocum considered what Slade was telling him. He'd said "we," so he had someone with him. How many? Not many, Slocum guessed. Slade wasn't the kind who'd share his bounty.

"Why not just gun me down from ambush, Slade?" called Slocum. "That's more your style." He wanted to rile the man, to get him angry enough to make a mistake. "I reckon I shouldn't have expected anything more than backshooting from your kind."

"My kind?" bellowed Slade. The gunman stepped out from the side of the carriage house, his six-shooter drawn and aimed at Slocum. "My kind's gonna give your ears to Hearst!"

Slocum had his target. He fell face forward, using part of the porch railing to shield him. As he dropped he drew. Landing hard on his belly ruined Slocum's aim, but the bullet he sent in Slade's direction made the gunman miss with his shot.

The shotgun blast from his left caused Slocum to roll and fire three quick shots. One round caught Slade's partner in the eye. The man let out a strangled cry and clutched at his head. He sank from sight, and Slocum knew he wouldn't be bushwhacking anyone again.

"I'm gonna kill you for what you done to me, Slocum." Slade's bullets tore up the porch all around Slocum. He got to his feet and dodged the gunman's last rounds as he sprinted for the far side of the carriage house.

"Come get me, Slade. If you've got the guts." Slocum checked his Colt Navy and saw that he had two rounds left. Not enough. He reached into the pocket of his duster and pulled out a freshly loaded cylinder. He knocked the old one from his gun and dropped in the new. Six shots now awaited Slade instead of just two.

"Come out and face me like a man, Slocum. You ain't got no more guts than a snake does hips," Slade called.

Slocum knew better than to step out and face the man. He'd be walking into a bullet. Slade had no intention of making it a fair fight. Slocum ducked low and swung around, getting off two shots. Neither came close to hitting Slade, who hunkered down behind the chopping block.

The gunman stood and came forward, his six-shooter aimed square at Slocum's head. "Don't go runnin' off, Slocum. I been counting your rounds. You're out of ammo. Now, what do I do with you? Cut you down like the toad you are, or—"

Slocum didn't let Slade go on. He fired once, twice, a third time. All three slugs found a target. Slocum was never sure which round it was that tore fairly through Slade's heart, nor did it much matter to him. The gunman dropped to the ground like a marionette with its strings cut. That was good enough.

Slocum used the toe of his boot to roll Slade onto his back. The man had died with a sneer on his face. It seemed fitting that anyone who might go to his funeral would remember him that way.

The gunfire had brought unwanted attention to the Hamilton house. Slocum backed off, then dashed to his horse. He had to pull the gelding away from the trough of oats.

"You've had enough for today," Slocum said. The horse shied, obviously not agreeing. Slocum put his spurs to the horse's flanks to get it moving at a gallop. He kept up the breakneck pace until he was over the divide, putting Virginia City on the other side of Mount Davidson. Only then did he slow to a walk and let the horse get back its wind. As they walked along, Slocum's keen eyes studied the dirt tracks in the back road.

"She came by not too long ago," Slocum said to himself. The dust hadn't worked back into the grooves cut by the carriage wheels, putting Belle less than an hour ahead. Slocum doubted she was making good time with such a heavily laden carriage. If she didn't leave this path, he'd overtake her by midday.

Slocum had to admit Belle had made better time than he'd thought. It.wasn't until two that he caught sight of a carriage pulled off the road and partially hidden by a stand of lodgepole pines. The horse pulling the carriage was drinking noisily from a stream. Belle and Corey held the animal to keep it from drinking too much.

"That's smart," Slocum said, walking up on them. Both women jumped in surprise. "Too much water'll make your mare bloat something fierce."

"John!" cried Belle Flowers. She put her hand to her mouth in a gesture Slocum associated with society ladies.

When he saw it, his hand flashed to his six-shooter. He drew and aimed it directly at Corey, who was fishing in her purse.

"Bring your hand out real slow, Corey," he ordered. "I want to see what you're so eager to find there."

She pulled out a double-barreled derringer.

"Just toss it into the stream. Don't worry none about scaring the fishes. This water's so dirty with filth from Parrish's Mill, there aren't many still alive."

Slocum holstered his Colt when the woman obeyed.

"John, you've got this all wrong," Belle started.

"Shut up, sister," snapped Corey. "Don't you see he knows everything? Why else is he here? It's surely not *your* charms." Corey batted her eyelashes and smiled sweetly. "He might be here for mine, though. He did enjoy them back in Virginia City."

Slocum saw the flash of anger that crossed Belle's face. The sisters didn't tell each other everything. Corey hadn't mentioned the time they'd spent together.

"Oh, Belle, you didn't think you'd keep him all to yourself? Tell me, John, which of us gave you more pleasure?"

Slocum ignored Corey. "I figured out most of your swindle. There's just one thing I have to know. How did you profit by making it look as if I'd bought the Cuckoo Clock Mine?"

Belle relaxed a mite and laughed. "I do declare, that's the easy part, John darling. I swindled them just as they did my poor father, except they called it legal."

"What are you talking about?"

Belle's expression hardened. "Hearst and the others. They robbed my father of his claims. Obadiah Clark was a damned claim jumper, but Hearst stole legally. All their lawyers and bought judges and disputed boundary claims—they *stole* from him, John. And I got some of it back."

"We did, Belle, *we* did," corrected Corey. "She is right about how Hearst robbed Papa. He was a good prospector but a terrible businessman. They held out all that wealth and it blinded him. It was easier than shearing a spring lamb." The bitterness in Corey's voice wasn't contrived.

"All right, so Hearst and the others in Consolidated Virginia stole what rightly belonged to your father. I'll even grant you that Clark was a claim jumper—"

"He was, the lowdown snake in the grass!" raged Belle.

"How did you profit by making it seem you'd sold the Cuckoo Clock to me?"

Belle laughed. "We were going to cut you in, John. Really."

Slocum would sooner believe the sun would come up in the west tomorrow morning. He said nothing, though, and nodded for her to go on spinning her yarn. He was curious to know how the swindle worked.

"Hearst thought you'd bought the mine after convincing Hanrahan it was worthless. No one in the Consolidated Virginia Company enjoys being cheated out of a prize," said Belle. "When we sent that picture ore to Parrish's Mill word had to get back to Hearst that you'd done him out of the biggest find in the entire Comstock Lode."

"Where did the ore come from?" asked Slocum.

"We needed the money from selling the Spit Bucket and the Silver Canary to buy the best we could find. We had it hauled in all the way from Tonopah so's nobody here would know. They'd think it came from the Cuckoo Clock."

Slocum nodded. "So you hornswoggled Hearst into thinking I'd done him out of the mine. How did you make anything off that?"

Corey laughed. "There's no honor among thieves, John, or among mine owners. We went to each of the partners in Consolidated Virginia—"

"And Consolidated California," Belle cut in, naming the other large stock company owning damned near everything in the Comstock Lode that Consolidated Virginia didn't. "We went to each partner and quietly sold them shares in your mine. It's the way business is done here."

Slocum knew that was true. Shares in Consolidated Virginia traded on the San Francisco stock exchange as if the pieces of paper were worth something. Shares in the Cuckoo Clock might fetch an attractive amount of money, if each thought someone had paid eight hundred thousand for the mine—and the assay played out at $4000 a ton. Since Lawrence Parrish was one of their own and had no reason to lie, they'd accept the value without question.

Especially if they thought they were gaining a march on the other partners.

Belle and Corey would have had them snapping to buy the bogus shares like coyotes fighting over a rabbit. Then another question hit him.

"How much of the mine did you sell this way?"

Belle laughed and it was with genuine enjoyment. "You are clever, John. That's one thing I like about you." She eyed him suggestively before she went on. "Between us, Corey and I sold the Cuckoo Clock five times over. Why, Parrish himself bought forty-nine percent for two hundred thousand and a contract to do all the smelting for free."

Slocum understood now. The women hadn't tried to sell the mine outright. By doling out large chunks, the men they swindled thought they were being cut in on a new bonanza. And Parrish would have jumped at the chance to own almost half an eight-hundred-thousand-dollar mine for such a price. Trading milling and smelting for the remainder was good business since he didn't have to pony up the cash.

"How much?" Slocum asked. "How much did You get from all of them?"

Belle and Corey looked at each other, trying to figure out how much to lie. Belle licked her lips and answered.

"Most of it is in San Francisco bank accounts. Even with so much gold and silver in Virginia City, they don't keep much cash around."

Slocum remembered the stacks of greenbacks Hearst had

used to pay for the two mines. He didn't believe them for an instant.

"What do you ladies have that's weighing down your carriage?" Slocum went over. The expressions of disgust on their faces told him they might not be telling the full truth. Some of the money might have been transferred to bank accounts, and he didn't believe all the swindled money was going into San Francisco banks. Too many of the partners in Consolidated Virginia owned banks there. But he suspected Belle and Corey had ridden out of Virginia City with a goodly amount in the rear of their carriage.

He reached for a tarp thrown over several boxes when a small detail he had overlooked clicked in his head. Slocum swung away from the carriage, his hand flashing to his Colt. He drew and fired just as Reed Flowers stepped out from behind a tree at the edge of the clearing. Belle and Corey's brother jerked and fell backward, his six-gun flying from his hand.

"I didn't know he was going to try shooting you, John," pleaded Belle, staring at the smoking pistol in Slocum's hand.

"Like hell," sniffed Corey. "She told him to wait over there and gun down anyone who might happen on us while we watered the horse. I told her it was silly."

Slocum didn't see any sorrow for their dead brother. What little he had seen of Reed Flowers explained that. He was a wastrel and a ne'er-do-well, and they had used him as they used everyone else.

Slocum said nothing as Belle prattled on about her innocence. He pulled back the tarp and revealed four large strongboxes.

"Keys?" he asked.

Corey smiled in her mock guileless way and fished out a necklace with two keys dangling from it. Belle drew out two more from a similar chain around her neck.

"We can be partners, John. This is only the start. We work well together. We can use this as seed money to get

the really big fish on our line." Belle kept up a running
description of what she and Slocum could do, if only they'd
team up.

"I need you, John. Now that Reed's gone, I need someone
to protect me."

Slocum almost laughed. Belle needed someone protecting her as much as a sidewinder needed shoes. He opened
the four strongboxes and simply stared. Two were packed
with gold dust. The other two held more greenbacks than
he'd ever seen in his life.

"Partners, John. We can be—"

Corey cut off her sister. "Shut up, Belle. He's not buying
any of it because you don't have anything to offer him.
Not like me. I can give you more than just money, John,
so much more."

She started for him but he held her at bay with a motion
of his six-shooter. She was as dangerous as her sister.

"You're not going to take our money," protested Belle,
changing her argument. "We risked everything for it. We
deserve it. Our papa was—"

"I'm only taking this one," Slocum said, swinging one
strongbox containing greenbacks from the carriage. He
looked longingly at the gold dust but knew he couldn't
weigh down his gelding and hope to make any time. If
he had a pack mule, the women would have been left
with nothing more than their dead brother to bury, but
fate worked in strange ways.

"Together, John, the three of us. You and Corey and I—"
Belle started for him again. He cocked the pistol and aimed
it square between her eyes.

"I've got a bounty on my head, thanks to you," he said
coldly. "I might have been killed any of a dozen times, and
you would have ridden off without giving me one damned
cent. Leaving you this much is more than you deserve."

He backed off, watching the women to make sure they
didn't try to go for other hidden weapons. Corey stood with
her hip cocked forward and her chest puffed up. She licked

her lips and still managed to look innocent. He knew what she was promising him if he stayed.

And Belle . . .

She looked so appealing, so lovely, so dangerous.

Slocum went to his horse and stuffed the greenbacks into his saddlebags. He barely had enough room for it all. He tossed the empty strongbox aside and mounted. Belle and Corey still beckoned to him—and truth to tell, he found them almost irresistible.

Almost.

He rode due north, thinking he might find a trail in that direction that would take him far, far away from the Flowers sisters and their conniving ways.